張瑜凌 編著

超簡單的旅遊英語

國家圖書館出版品預行編目資料

超簡單的旅遊英語 / 張瑜凌編著
-- 二版. -- 新北市 : 雅典文化, 民107.02
面 ; 公分. -- (全民學英文 ; 47)
ISBN 978-986-5753-97-9(平裝附光碟片)
1.英語 2.旅遊 3.會話
805.188 106023542

全民學英文系列 47

超簡單的旅遊英語

責任編輯／張瑜凌
內文排版／王國卿
封面設計／姚恩涵

法律顧問：方圓法律事務所／涂成樞律師

總經銷：永續圖書有限公司
永續圖書線上購物網
www.foreverbooks.com.tw

CVS代理／美璟文化有限公司
TEL：(02)2723-9968
FAX：(02)2723-9668

出版日／2018年02月

雅典文化

出版社
22103 新北市汐止區大同路三段194號9樓之1
TEL (02)8647-3663
FAX (02)8647-3660

序文　出國不再比手畫腳

出國最害怕什麼？

是不是通關時不曉得如何和機場人員溝通？

是不是購物時不知道如何表達自己的需求？

是不是觀光時不知道如何買票？

是不是搭車時不知道如何轉車？

是不是害怕自己迷路了？

以上的問題都是在你不會說英文的情況下才會發生的。但是不會說英文難道就不能出國自助旅行、觀光、出差、唸書嗎？「超簡單的旅遊英語」能幫您解決了上述所有問題。

「超簡單的旅遊英語」包含以下單元：

Unit 01搭飛機

Unit 02旅館住宿

Unit 03飲食

Unit 04速食店點餐

Unit 05購物

Unit 06搭乘交通工具

Unit 07觀光

Unit 08尋求協助

Unit 09和警察的互動

Unit 10發生意外報案

Unit 11交通事故

每一個單元都有最簡單實用的情境會話，以及相關的類似說法：「你還可以這麼說」以及「對方也可以這麼說」，只要根據您的需求尋找目錄上標示的情境主題，您就可以輕鬆搞定英文。

Unit 1 搭飛機

Unit 2 旅館住宿

Unit 3 飲食

Unit 4 速食店點餐

Unit 5 購物

Unit 6 搭乘交通工具

Unit 7 觀光

Unit 8 尋求協助

Unit 9 和警察的互動

Unit 10 發生意外報案

Unit 11 交通事故

500

Unit 1 搭飛機

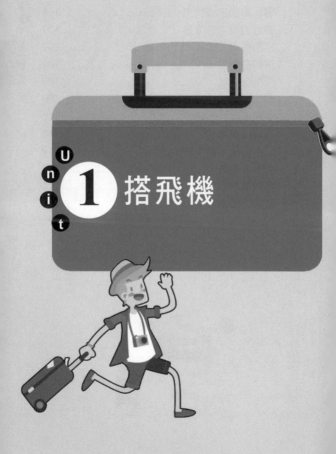

▶ 機票

問 Good morning. This is Chinese Airlines.
早安。這是中華航空。

答 I want to make a reservation from Taipei to Dallas.
我要預約從台北到達拉斯的機票。

你還可以這麼說:

► I would like to book two seats from Taipei to New York on August 25th.
我要訂兩個人八月廿五日從台北到紐約的機票。

▶ 票價

問 How much is the airfare?
機票多少錢？

答 It's two thousand dollars.
兩千元。

對方可以這麼說:

▶ I would like to know the airfare.

我想要知道票價。

▶ What's the one-way fare?

單程票價是多少錢？

▶ What's the fare from Taipei to Tokyo?

從台北到東京票價是多少錢？

▶ 行程

問 I'd like to book the first flight to New York for May 1st.

我想預訂五月一日到紐約的最早航班。

答 OK, sir.

好的，先生。

你還可以這麼說:

▶ Do you fly to New York on September 2nd?

你們有九月二日到東京的班機嗎？

▶ Do you fly from Taipei to Tokyo on September 2nd?

你們有九月二日從台北到紐約的班機嗎？

▶ 訂機位

問 There's a flight at 9 am and one at 11 am.

早上九點有一班，還有一班是十一點。

答 I would like the 9 am one.

我要九點的那一個班次。

你還可以這麼說:

- I would like a nonstop flight.

  我要訂直達的班機。

- I would like to book a round-trip ticket.

  我要訂一張來回機票。

- I would like to book two seats.

  我要訂兩張機票。

- I prefer a morning flight.

  我偏好早上的班機。

▶ 直達航班

問 I'd like to book a nonstop flight from New York to Paris.
我想預訂從紐約到巴黎的直達航班。

答 What time do you prefer?
您偏好什麼時間？

▶ 轉機航班

➪ I would like a stop-over flight.
我要訂需要轉機的班機。

➪ I would like a stop-over flight to Los Angeles.
我要訂到洛杉磯的轉機班機。

➪ I prefer to stop over in Hong Kong.
我比較喜歡在香港轉機。

➪ I'm thinking of flying from Paris to Seattle on May 1st and from Seattle to Tokyo on May 8th.
我打算五月一日從巴黎到西雅圖，五月八日從西雅圖到東京。

▶ 取消機位

問 I want to cancel my reservation.

我想取消我的訂位。

答 OK, sir. May I have your name?

好的，先生。請問您的大名？

▶ 變更機位

問 I would like to change my flight.

我想變更我的班機。

答 No problem, madam.

沒問題，女士。

▶ 航班查詢

問 Which flight would you prefer?

您想要那一個班次？

答 Could you please find another flight before May 1st?

請你替我找五月一日之前的另一個班機好嗎？

你還可以這麼說:

▶ Are there two seats available on the 2 pm flight?

兩點起飛的飛機還有兩個空位嗎？

▶ Do you fly to New York on next Monday?

你們有下星期一到紐約的班機嗎？

▶ Could you check the boarding time for me?

你能替我查班機時刻表嗎？

▶ 確認機位

問 I would like to reconfirm a flight.

我要確認機位。

答 OK, sir. Your name, please.

好的，先生。您的大名？

你還可以這麼說:

▶ I'd like to reconfirm a flight for Mr. White.

我想替懷特先生再確認機位。

▶ 詢有關辦理報到的問題

問 Can I check in now?
我現在可以辦理登機嗎？

答 OK, sir. Passport and visa, please.
好的，先生。請給我護照和簽證。

你還可以這麼說:

▶ Can I check in for CA Flight 546?

我可以辦理CA546班登機嗎？

▶ Where may I check in for United Airlines Flight 706?

我應該在哪裡辦理聯合航空 706 班機的登機手續？

▶ What time should I have to be at the airport?

我應該什麼時候到機場？

▶ 辦理報到

問 Check-in, please.
我要辦理登機。

答 Passport, please.
請給我護照。

你 還可以這麼說:

► I would like to check in.

我要辦理登機。

► 要求特定機位

問 Is it an aisle seat?

這是靠走道的座位嗎？

答 No, it's not. It's a window seat.

不，這不是。這是靠窗的座位。

你 還可以這麼說:

► May I have a window seat?

我可以要靠窗戶的座位嗎？

► I don't want the aisle seat.

我不要走道的位子。

► I want an aisle seat, please.

我想要一個走道的位子。

► I want the first class seat.

我想要頭等艙的座位。

▶ 行李托運

問 I have baggage to be checked.
我有行李要托運。

答 Please put it on the scale.
請把它放在秤上。

你還可以這麼說:

▶ I have two suitcases.
我有兩件行李箱。

▶ Can I carry this bag with me?
我可以隨身帶這個袋子嗎？

▶ How many suitcases can I take on a China flight?
搭乘中國航空的班機我可帶多少行李箱？

▶ 行李超重費用

問 How much is the extra charge?
超重費是多少？

答 You have to pay two hundred for excess baggage.
那些超重的行李你要付兩百元。

你還可以這麼說:

► What are your charges for excess baggage?

你們的行李超重費是多少？

► 出境登機

➩ I am on a USA Airlines flight.

我要搭乘美國航空公司。

➩ What time will boarding start?

什麼時候開始登機？

➩ What's the boarding time?

登機時間是什麼時候？

➩ Is the flight on time?

班機準時起飛嗎？

► 登機處

➩ Excuse me, where should I board?

請問，我應該到哪裡登機？

➩ Where is the boarding gate?

登機門在哪裡？

➪ I don't know where I should board.
我不知道我應該在哪裡登機。

▶ 走錯登機門

問 May I help you?
需要我幫忙嗎？

答 I think I am at the wrong gate.
我想我走錯登機門了。

▶ 詢問轉機

➪ Where can I get information on a connecting flight?
我可以到哪裡詢問轉機的事？

➪ How should I transfer?
我要如何轉機？

➪ How do I transfer to Washington?
我要如何轉機到華盛頓？

▶ 轉機

➪ I am in transit.
我要轉機。

➩ I am in transit to Paris.
我要轉機到巴黎。

➩ I am connecting with CA651.
我要轉搭CA651班機。

▶ 過境

➩ How long will we stop here?
我們會在這裡停留多久？

➩ How long is the stopover?
過境要停留多久？

➩ I am a transit passenger for Flight UA356.
我是要搭乘美國航班356號的轉機乘客。

➩ I am continuing on to Washington.
我要繼續前往華盛頓。

▶ 行李提領的好幫手

➩ Could you help me get my baggage down?
你可以幫我把我的行李拿下來嗎？

➩ Where can I get a baggage cart?
哪裡有行李推車？

▶ 行李提領

問 Where can I get my baggage?
我可以在哪裡提領行李？

答 Your baggage is on the conveyer.
你的行李在行李傳輸帶上。

你還可以這麼說:

▶ Is this the baggage claim area from USA Airlines 561?
這是美國航空561班機的行李提領處嗎？

▶ Can I get my baggage now?
我可以現在提領我的行李嗎？

▶ Excuse me, sir, but that is my baggage.
先生，抱歉，那是我的行李。

▶ 行李遺失

➪ I don't see my baggage.
我沒有看見我的行李了。

➪ I can't find my baggage. What can I do?
我找不到我的行李。我應該怎麼辦？

➪ One of my bags hasn't come.
我的一件行李沒有出來。

▶ 詢找行李遺失申報處

問 Where is the Lost Baggage Service?
行李遺失申報處在哪裡？

答 It's over there.
在那裡。

你還可以這麼說:

▶ Where can I find the Lost Baggage Service.
我可以在哪裡找到行李遺失申報處？

▶ Do you know where the Lost Baggage Service is?
你知道行李遺失申報處在哪裡嗎？

▶ 登記行李遺失

問 I think two pieces of my baggage have been lost.
我覺得我的兩件行李遺失了。

答 Please fill out this claim form.
請填這張申訴表格。

▶ 形容遺失行李的外觀

問 Can you tell me the features of your baggage?
你能形容一下你行李的外觀嗎？

答 It is a medium-sized, and it is black.
中等尺寸，黑色的。

▶ 解決遺失行李的方法

➪ How long will you find it?
你們要多久才會找到？

➪ What if you couldn't find my baggage?
萬一你們找不到我的行李怎麼辦？

➪ Will you inform me as soon as you find them?
你們找到它們的時候，可以立刻通知我嗎？

➪ Please deliver my baggage to this address.
請將我的行李送到這個地址。

▶ 詢問是否可以兌換貨幣

➪ Where is the currency exchange?
貨幣兌換處在哪裡？

➪ Can I exchange money here?
我可以在這裡兌換錢幣嗎？

➪ Could you cash a traveler's check?
你可以把旅行支票換成現金嗎？

▶ 兌換成零錢

問 Could you give me some small change with it?
你能把這些兌換為小面額零錢嗎？

答 How much would you like to exchange?
您要換成多少？

你還可以這麼說:

► Would you please break this bill?

能請您將這張紙鈔找開嗎？

▶ 兌換成零錢的數目

問 How much do you want to exchange?
你想兌換多少？

答 Can you make me change for this bill?
這張鈔票能找得開嗎？

你 還可以這麼說:

► Can you exchange a dollar for ten dimes?
你能把一美元換成十個一角的銀幣嗎？

► I want to break this 200 dollars into 4 twenties, 3 tens and the rest in coins.
我想要將兩百元兌換成四張二十元、三張十元，剩下的是硬幣。

► Could you include some small change?
可以包括一些零錢嗎？

▶ 兌換幣值

問 What currency do you want to convert from?
你想要用哪一種貨幣兌換？

答 Could you change this into U.S. dollars?
你可以把這個兌換為美元嗎？

你還可以這麼說:

► How much in dollars is that?
（兌換）美元是多少？

► I want to exchange money into New Taiwan dollars.
我想要兌換成新台幣。

► I'd like to exchange some U.S. dollars to German Marks.
我要把一些美金兌換成德國馬克。

► I'd like to change NT$10,000 into U.S. dollars.
我要把一萬元台幣換成美金。

► 幣值匯率

問 What's the exchange rate?
匯率是多少？

答 The exchange rate from U.S. dollar to New Taiwan dollar is thirty-four point five.
現在美金兌換成新台幣的匯率是卅四點五。

你還可以這麼說:

► What is the exchange rate now?

現在匯率是多少？

► Could you tell me the procedures and the exchange rate?

你能告訴我手續和匯率嗎？

► 機場常見問題

➩ Could you page my child for me?
可以幫我廣播呼叫我的孩子嗎？

➩ Do you have maps of the downtown?
你們有市中心的地圖嗎？

➩ Is there a free city map?
有沒有免費的城市地圖？

➩ How can I get to Four Seasons Hotel?
我要怎麼去四季飯店？

➩ How much does it cost to downtown by taxi?
坐計程車到市中心要多少錢？

➩ Where should I catch a bus?
我要在哪裡搭公車？

➩ Does anyone here speak Chinese?
這裡有沒有會說中文的人？

▶ 證件查驗

問 May I see your passport and visa, please?
請給我您的護照和簽證。

答 This is my passport and visa.
這是我的護照和簽證。

你還可以這麼說:

▶ I couldn't find my visa.

我找不到我的簽證。

▶ 通關

問 Are you traveling alone?
你自己來旅遊的嗎？

答 Yes, I am alone.
是的，我一個人（來的）。

你還可以這麼說:

▶ I am with my parents.

我和我父母一起來的。

▶ I am with a travel tour.

我是跟團的。

▶ 入境原因

問 What's the purpose of your visit?
你此行的目的是什麼？

答 It's for business.
我是來出差的。

你還可以這麼說:

▶ I am here for sightseeing/touring.

我來這裡觀光/旅行。

▶ I am here for studies.

我來唸書的。

▶ Just touring.

只是旅遊。

▶ I am just passing through.

我只是路過。

▶ 停留時間

問 How long are you going to stay in England?
您要在英國停留多久？

答 I want to stay here for about 8 days.
我大約會在這裡停留八天。

你還可以這麼說:

▶ I will stay here for one more week.
我會在這裡留一個多星期。

▶ It's about 3 weeks.
大概三個星期。

▶ 檢查攜帶的隨身物品

問 Why do you take them with you?
你為什麼帶這些東西？

答 Just personal belongings.
只是個人用品。

你還可以這麼說:

- Those medicines are prepared for this tour.

這些藥物是為了這趟旅行而準備的。

- They are just some souvenirs.

它們只是一些紀念品。

- Personal stuff.

私人物品。

▶ 申報商品

問 Do you have anything to declare?
有沒有要申報的物品？

答 No, I have nothing to declare.
沒有，我沒有要申報的物品。

你還可以這麼說:

- Yes, there are four bottles of wine.

有的，我有四瓶酒。

▶ 沒收攜帶物品

問 I have to confiscate all your stuff.
我必須沒收所有你的東西。

答 Can't I bring them in?
我不能帶這些進來？

▶ 詢問是否攜帶違禁品

問 Do you have any prohibited items?
有沒有攜帶任何違禁品？

答 No, I don't.
沒有，我沒有帶。

▶ 繳交稅款

問 You have to pay duty on the excess.
你要付超重費。

答 How much is the duty on this?
這個要付多少稅金呢？

你還可以這麼說:

▶ How much is the duty?

稅金是多少？

▶ How much did you say?

你說是多少？

▶ How should I pay for it?

我應該要如何付呢？

▶ 找不到機位

問 I couldn't find my seat.
我找不到我的座位。

答 Let me see your ticket.
讓我看看你的機票。

▶ 帶位

問 Would you please take me to my seat?
能請你幫我帶位嗎？

答 Down this aisle. It's on your right.
順著走道，在你的右手邊。

你還可以這麼說:

► Could you show me where my seat is?

你能告訴我我的座位在哪裡嗎？

► 確認機位

問 My seat is 32L.

我的機位是是32L。

答 Go straight ahead, and you will see it on your left.

先直走，你就會看到在你的左手邊。

對方可以這麼說:

► OK. It's a window seat on the left.

好的，是個在左邊靠窗的位子。

► 換機位

問 Can I change my seat?

我能不能換座位？

答 I am afraid not.

不要。

你還可以這麼說:

- Can you switch seats with me?

  你能和我和座位嗎？

- Can we move to the smoking area?

  我們能移到吸菸區嗎？

- I would like to move to the non-smoking area.

  我想要換位子到非吸煙區。

▶ 坐錯機位

問 Excuse me, but that's my seat.

抱歉，那是我的位子。

答 Sorry, my mistake.

抱歉，我坐錯了。

你還可以這麼說:

- I am afraid this is my seat.

  這個恐怕是我的座位。

- I think 32L is my seat.

  我覺得32L是我的座位。

▶ 飛機上的行李

問 Excuse me. Where should I put my baggage?
抱歉，我應該把我的行李放哪裡？

答 You can store extra baggage in the overhead cabinet.
你可以把多出來的行李放在上方的行李櫃裡。

▶ 繫緊安全帶

問 How do I fasten my seat-belt?
我要怎麼繫緊我的安全帶？

答 Let me show you.
我示範給你看。

▶ 詢問空服員問題

➪ Would you do me a favor?
你能幫我一個忙嗎？

➪ Would you put this in the overhead bin?
您可以幫我把它放進櫃子裡嗎？

➪ Where is the lavatory?
盥洗室在哪裡？

➪ Can I recline my seat back now?
我現在可以將椅背往後靠嗎？

➪ May I smoke now?
我現在可以抽菸嗎？

➪ When can I buy some duty-free perfumes?
我什麼時候可以買免稅香水？

➪ What is the local time in the USA?
美國當地時間是幾點鐘？

▶ 尋求空服員協助提供物品

問 I feel cold. May I have a blanket?
我覺得有一些冷，我能要一條毯子嗎？

答 Sure. Would you also like a pillow?
好的，你要不要枕頭？

你還可以這麼說:

► Do you have a Chinese newspaper?

你們有中文報紙嗎？

▶ May I have a pack of playing cards?

可以給我一副撲克牌嗎？

▶ May I have a headset?

可以給我一副耳機嗎？

▶ May I have a glass of water?

我可以要一杯水嗎？

▶ 協助操作機器

問 How do I turn this light on?

我要怎麼打開這個燈？

答 Let me help you with this.

我來幫您。

你還可以這麼說:

▶ How do I operate this?

這個我要怎麼操作？

▶ It doesn't work.

這個不能運轉。

▶ 用餐時間

問 What time will we have a meal served?
我們幾點用餐？

答 About 7 o'clock.
大約七點鐘。

▶ 詢問餐點選擇

問 What would you like for dinner?
晚餐您想吃什麼？

答 What do you have?
你們有什麼（餐點）？

▶ 選擇餐點

問 What would you like for dinner?
晚餐您想吃什麼？

答 I would like beef, please.
我要吃牛肉，謝謝。

你還可以這麼說:

► Do you have a vegetarian meal?

你們有素食餐點嗎？

► Do you have instant noodlea?

你們有泡麵嗎？

► 選擇飲料

問 And you, sir? Coffee or tea?
先生您呢？咖啡或茶？

答 Coffee, please.
請給我咖啡。

你還可以這麼說:

► May I have some more tea, please?

我能再多要點茶嗎？

► 要求提供飲料

問 May I have a glass of water, please?
我能要一杯水嗎？

答 OK. I will be right back with you.

好的，我馬上回來。

你還可以這麼說:

► Can I have some coffee?

我可以喝一些咖啡嗎？

► May I have a glass of orange juice?

我能要一杯柳橙汁嗎？

► May I have something to drink?

我能喝點飲料嗎？

► I am a little thirsty. Do you have any cold drinks?

我有一點口渴，你們有任何冷飲嗎？

► May I have a glass of hot water? Not too hot, please.

我可以要一杯熱開水嗎？不要太熱。

▶ 在飛機上覺得不舒服

問 You look terrible.

你看起來氣色不太好。

答 I don't feel well.

我覺得不舒服。

你還可以這麼說:

▶ I feel airsick.

我覺得暈機。

▶ I feel like vomiting.

我想吐。

▶ I have a pain here.

我這裡痛。

▶ Do you have airsickness bags?

你有嘔吐袋嗎？

▶ 在飛機上生病

問 Are you OK, sir?

先生，您還好吧？

答 I need a doctor.

我需要醫生。

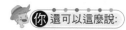

你還可以這麼說:

▶ I have a headache.

我頭痛。

▶ I have a stomachache.

我胃痛。

▶ I have a fever.

我發燒了。

Unit 2 旅館住宿

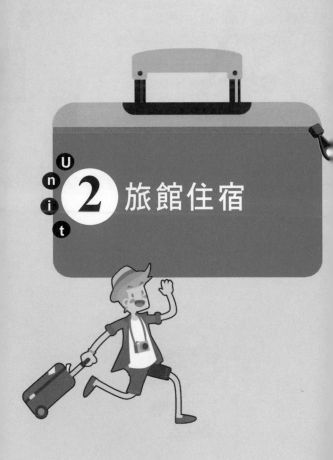

▶ 詢問空房

問 Do you have a twin-bedded room?
你們有兩張單人床的房間嗎？

答 Yes, we do.
是的，我們有。

你 還可以這麼說:

▶ Do you have a single room?

你們有單人房嗎？

▶ Do you have a double room?

你們有床人床的房間嗎？

▶ 旅館客滿

問 Do you have a twin available?
你們有兩張單人床的房間嗎？

答 I am sorry, sir, but we are all booked up.
抱歉，先生，我們全部客滿了。

▶ 訂房

問 We have a double room available.

我們目前有一個雙人床房間。

答 OK. I will take it.

好，我要訂。

你還可以這麼說:

▶ I'd like a room for one.

我要一間單人房。

▶ I'd like a room for two with separate beds.

我要一間有兩張床的雙人房間。

▶ 推薦其他飯店

問 Could you recommend another hotel?

你可以推薦另一個飯店嗎？

答 Yes. There is another hotel at the First Street.

好的。在第一街有另一家飯店。

你還可以這麼說:

▶ Are there any hotels around here?

這附近還有沒有旅館？

▶ 詢問房價

問 How much per night?

（住宿）一晚要多少錢？

答 4 hundred dollars per night.

一晚要四百元。

你還可以這麼說:

▶ How much will it be?

要多少錢？

▶ How much should I pay for a week?

一個星期得付多少錢？

▶ Do you have any cheaper rooms?

你們有便宜一點的房間嗎？

▶ How much for a single room?

單人房多少錢？

▶ 房價包括的項目

問 Are there any meals included?

有包括餐點嗎？

答 Yes, sir.

有的先生。

你還可以這麼說:

▶ Does the room rate include breakfast?

住宿費有包括早餐嗎？

▶ Does it include tax?

有含稅嗎？

▶ 登記住宿

問 May I help you, sir?

先生，需要我幫忙嗎？

答 I would like to check in.

我要登記住宿。

你還可以這麼說:

► I have a reservation for 2 nights.

我已訂了兩天住宿。

► Here is the confirmation slip.

這是我的確認單。

► 詢問登記住宿的時間

問 What time can I check in?

我什麼時候可以登記住宿？

答 Anytime after 11 am.

早上十一點之後都可以。

你還可以這麼說:

► When is the check-in time?

什麼時候可以登記住宿？

► 詢問是否預約登記住宿

問 Did you make a reservation?

您有預約住宿嗎？

答 Yes, I have a reservation. My name is Tom Jones.

有的，我有預約訂房。我的名字是湯姆·瓊斯。

你還可以這麼說:

► No, I didn't make a reservation.

沒有，我沒有預約。

► 房間的樓層

問 What's the floor?

在幾樓？

答 On the third floor.

在三樓。

► 飯店用餐

問 This is your breakfast coupon.

這是您的早餐券。

答 What time is breakfast served?

早餐什麼時候供應？

你還可以這麼說:

► Where should I go to for the breakfast?

我應該去哪用餐？

► 沒有早餐券

問 I forgot to bring breakfast coupons with me.

我忘了帶早餐券。

答 It doesn't matter. Just tell me your room number.

沒關係。只要告訴我房號就好。

你還可以這麼說:

► I lost my breakfasts coupon.

我把早餐券弄丟了。

► 表明身分

問 What's your room number?

您的房號是幾號？

答 I am Jack Smith of Room 618.

我是618號房的傑克・史密斯

你還可以這麼說:

► This is Room 206.

這是206號房。

► My room number is 300.

我的房間號碼是300。

► 提供房間鑰匙

問 Room 756. Key, please.

房號756。請給我鑰匙。

答 Here you are, sir.

先生，在這裡。

你還可以這麼說:

► Key to Room 756, please.

我要拿房號756的鑰匙。

► My room number is 756.

我的房間號碼是756。

▶ 早上叫醒服務

問 Give me a wake-up call at eight, please.
請在八點打電話叫醒我。

答 Yes, sir.
好的，先生。

你還可以這麼說:

▶ I'd like a wake-up call every morning.
我每一天都要早上叫醒(的服務)。

▶ Could I have an early morning call, please?
我能有早上叫醒的服務嗎？

▶ 客房服務

問 May I help you, sir?
先生，有什麼需要我服務的？

答 I'd like an extra pillow for Room 504.
我要在504房多加一個枕頭。

你還可以這麼說:

► Would you bring us a bottle of champagne?

你能帶一瓶香檳給我們嗎？

► Let's see, and I want a chicken sandwich.

我想想，還有我要一份雞肉三明治。

► I can't find any towels in my room.

我的房裡沒有毛巾。

► Could you bring some towels right now?

請你馬上送幾條毛巾過來好嗎？

► 衣物送洗

問 Do you have the laundry service?

你們有洗衣服務嗎？

答 Please put it in the plastic bag and leave it on the bed.

請放在塑膠袋裡，然後放在床上。

你還可以這麼說:

► I have some laundry.

我有一些衣服要送洗。

► I'd like to send my suit to the cleaners.

我要把我的西裝送洗。

► 拿回送洗衣物

問 When can I have them returned?

我什麼時候可以拿回來？

答 By this afternoon.

下午之前就可以。

你還可以這麼說:

► I haven't gotten the coat back that I sent to the cleaners yesterday.

我昨天送洗的外套還沒送回來。

► From what time do you accept the laundry?

你們從什麼時候起受理送洗的衣物？

► 旅館設施出問題

➪ The lock of my room is broken.

房間的鎖壞了。

➪ The dryer doesn't work.

吹風機壞了。

➪ There is no hot water in my room.
我的房間裡沒有熱水。

➪ There is something wrong with the toilet.
馬桶有點問題。

➪ My phone is out of order.
我的電話故障了。

➪ The toilet in my room doesn't work properly.
我房間的廁所壞了。

➪ The toilet doesn't flush.
馬桶不能沖水了。

➪ I think the filament has broken.
我想燈絲壞了。

➪ The water doesn't drain.
水流不出來。

➪ We are out of the toilet paper.
我們沒有衛生紙了。

➪ The air conditioner doesn't work.
空調壞了。

▶ 在房間內打外線電話

問 How do I call a number outside this hotel?

我要怎麼從飯店撥外線出去？

答 Dial 9 first, and then the phone number.

先撥九，再撥電話號碼。

你還可以這麼說:

- Is this coin all right for telephones?

  這個硬幣可以打電話嗎？

- Could you connect me with the telephone directory assistance?

  可以幫我接查號台嗎？

▶ 詢問退房時間

問 When is the check-out time?

退房的時間是什麼時候？

答 Before 11 am.

早上十一點之前。

▶ 退房

問 Check out, please.

請結帳。

答 Yes, sir.

好的，先生。

你還可以這麼說:

▶ I would like to check out.

我要結帳。

▶ 結帳

問 How much does it charge?

這要收多少錢？

答 Your bill is twenty thousand dollars.

您的帳單是兩萬元。

你 還可以這麼說:

► Put it on my hotel bill, please.

請算在我的住宿費裡。

► Are there any additional charges?

是否有其他附加費用？

► 付帳方式

問 How would you like to pay it, sir?

先生，您要怎麼付錢呢？

答 I will pay cash.

我會付現金。

你 還可以這麼說:

► By credit card.

用信用卡付。

► Can I pay with a traveler's check?

我可以付旅行支票嗎？

▶ 帳單有問題

問 I am afraid there is something wrong with the bill.

帳單恐怕有點問題。

答 Sorry, sir. Let me take a look.

抱歉，先生。我看一看。

你還可以這麼說:

▶ Are the service charges and tax included?

是否包括服務費和稅金嗎？

▶ Something wrong with the bill.

帳單有點問題。

▶ 和櫃臺互動

問 How may I help you, sir?

先生，需要我幫忙嗎？

答 I'd like to change my room.

我想換房間。

你還可以這麼說:

► Where is the locker?

寄物櫃在哪裡？

► Do I have any messages?

我有任何的留言嗎？

► This is Mary Jones in Room 602. Do you have any messages for me?

我是 602 室的瑪莉·瓊斯。有沒有給我的留言？

► I have lost my room key.

我遺失了我的房間鑰匙了。

► I locked myself out.

我把自己反鎖在外面。

► Could you store my baggage?

請你幫我保管行李好嗎？

► I'd like to pick up my baggage.

我要拿行李。

► Could you call a taxi for me, please? I'm going to the airport.

請你幫我叫部計程車好嗎？我要去機場。

Unit 3 飲食

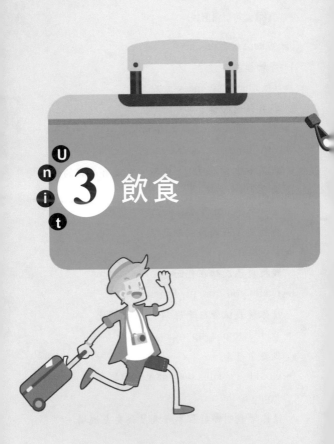

▶ 詢問營業時間

問 When does the restaurant open/close?
餐廳幾點營業/打烊？

答 The restaurant opens at 11 am.
餐廳早上十一點開始營業。

對方可以這麼說:

▶ The restaurant closes at 10 pm.
餐廳晚上十點打烊。

▶ The restaurant's hours are from 11 am until 10 pm.
餐廳的營業時間從早上十一點到晚上十點。

▶ 餐點的種類

問 What would you like for dinner?
你晚餐想吃什麼？

答 Let's eat sandwiches for dinner.
我們晚餐吃三明治吧！

你還可以這麼說:

▶ I want to eat hamburger.

我想吃漢堡。

▶ I want to have fried chicken.

我想要吃炸雞。

▶ I miss Chinese food.

我想念中華料理。

▶ 邀請用餐

問 Would you like to have dinner with us?
你想和我們一起用餐嗎？

答 We would love to, but we have other plans.
我們很想，但是我們有其他計畫。

▶ 回答是否要用餐

問 I am hungry.
我餓了。

答 Let's grab something to eat!
我們隨便找點東西吃吧！

你還可以這麼說:

► But I am not hungry at all.
可是我一點都不餓。

► I want to try something different.
我想要試一試一些不一樣的。

► I prefer to eat out.
我比較喜歡去外面用餐。

► 電話訂位

問 I want to make a reservation.
我想訂訂位。

答 What time, sir?
先生，(訂)什麼時間？

► 有事先訂位

問 Do you have a reservation?
你有訂位嗎？

答 Yes, I made a reservation at six.
有的，我訂了六點的位子。

你還可以這麼說:

► Yes. I made a reservation yesterday.

有的，我昨天有訂位。

► We had a reservation.

我們已經有預約。

► My reservation code is 756.

我的預約代號是756.

► 報上訂位姓名

問 Welcome to Century Restaurant.
歡迎光臨世紀餐廳。

答 We had a reservation. My name is Sophia Jones.
我們已經有預約。我的名字是蘇菲亞・瓊斯。

► 現場訂位

問 Welcome to Four Seasons Restaurant.
歡迎光臨四季餐廳。

答 I want to make a reservation for five people.
我想訂五個人的位子。

你還可以這麼說:

► I want a table for 2, please.
我要二個人的位子。

► There are 4 of us.
我們有四個人。

► 詢問用餐人數

問 How many persons, please?
請問有幾位？

答 Four.
四個人。

對方可以這麼說:

► How many people, please?
請問有幾位？

▶ 說明用餐人數

問 For how many, please?

您要訂幾人(的位子)?

答 I am alone.

我一個人。

你 還可以這麼說:

▶ For 5.

五個人。

▶ There are 4 of us.

我們有四個人。

▶ We are a group of 5.

我們有五個人。

▶ A table for 4, please.

四個人的位子。

▶ 詢問餐廳是否客滿

問 May I help you?

需要我效勞嗎?

答 Do you have a table available?

現在還有空位嗎?

你還可以這麼說:

▶ Can we have a table?

有空位給我們嗎？

▶ 餐廳客滿

問 Do you have a table available?

現在還有空位嗎？

答 I'm sorry, but we are quite full tonight.

很抱歉，今晚位子都滿了。

對方可以這麼說:

▶ It's booked up tonight.

今晚都客滿了。

▶ I'm afraid all our tables are taken.

恐怕我們所有的位子都坐滿了。

▶ I'm afraid we are fully booked for tonight.

今晚的席位恐怕已訂滿了。

▶ There are no tables now.

現在沒有座位。

▶ 詢問是否願意等空位

問 How long do we have to wait?

我們要等多久？

答 Would you mind waiting until one is free?

您介意等到有空位嗎？

對方可以這麼說:

▶ I am afraid you have to wait for 40 minutes. Is it OK?

您恐怕要等四十分鐘。可以嗎？

▶ I will call you when a table is free.

有空位時我再叫您。

▶ Would you mind waiting until then?

您要等到那時候嗎？

▶ Would you mind waiting for 30 minutes?

您介不介意等三十分鐘？

▶ 分開座位或併桌

問 Would you mind sitting separately?

您們介不介意分開坐嗎？

答 No, we don't mind.

不會，我不介意。

對方可以這麼說:

▶ Would you mind sharing a table?

您介不介意和其他人併桌？

▶ 等待服務生帶位

問 Are you being waiting on, sir?

先生，有人為您帶位嗎？

答 Yes, we have been waiting here for 30 minutes.

是的，我們已經等了卅分鐘了。

▶ 吸菸／非吸菸區

問 Where would you prefer to sit?

您喜歡那個位置？

答 Non-smoking, please.

非吸菸區。

你還可以這麼說:

► Smoking area. Thanks.

吸菸區，謝謝。

► It doesn't matter.

都可以。

► 等待座位安排

問 You have to wait for about 20 minutes for the non-smoking area.

要非吸菸區的話，你們大概要等廿分鐘。

答 That's all right. We can wait.

沒關係，我們可以等。

你還可以這麼說:

► We can wait.

我們可以等。

► It's too late.

太晚了。

▶ 服務生帶位

問 I'll show you to your table.

我帶您入座。

答 Thanks.

謝謝！

對方可以這麼說:

▶ This way, please.

這邊請。

▶ Watch your step.

請小心腳步。

▶ We have a table for you now.

我們現在有給您的空位了。

▶ I am sorry to have kept you waiting.

抱歉讓您久等了。

▶ We're very sorry for the delay.

非常抱歉耽擱您的時間。

▶ 服務生帶到位子上

問 How about this table, sir? The view here is great.

先生，這個位子如何？這裡的風景很棒。

答 OK. We like it.

好的，我們喜歡。

對方可以這麼說:

▶ What do you think of this seat, sir?

先生，您覺得這個位子如何？

▶ How do you like it, sir?

先生，您喜歡這個位子嗎？

▶ Is this fine with you?

這個位子好嗎？

▶ 座位偏好

問 Where would you prefer to sit, sir?

先生，您想坐哪裡？

答 How about over there?

那裡可以嗎？

你還可以這麼說:

► By the window, please.

請給我靠窗的座位。

► Not close to the gate.

不要離門口太近。

► By the window, if you have.

如果有的話，給我靠窗的座位。

► Just not close to the aisle.

只要不要靠近走道。

► Far away from the rest room.

離盥洗室遠一點。

► 指定座位區域

問 Please be seated.

請坐。

答 But we would like the seats near the window.

但是我們想要靠窗的位子。

你還可以這麼說:

► But I would like a table on the side.

但是我想要靠邊的位子。

► But I don't like this seat. It's too cold here.

但是我不喜歡這個位子。這裡太冷了。

► How about that seat at the corner?

角落的位子可以嗎？

► 不喜歡餐廳安排的座位

問 How about this area?

這一區呢？

答 I don't like this area.

我不喜歡這一區。

你還可以這麼說:

► I don't think so.

我不認為（這個座位好）。

► 自行指定座位

問 Excuse me, could we take these two seats?

抱歉，我們可以要這兩個位子嗎？

答 Sure. Please be seated.
當然可以，請坐。

你還可以這麼說:

► May I take this seat?

我可以坐這個位子嗎？

► May we have those two seats?

我們可以坐那兩個座位嗎？

► 要求安靜的座位

問 Could we have a quiet table?
我們能不能要安靜的座位?

答 I will arrange another table for you immediately.
我馬上為您安排另一個桌子。

你還可以這麼說:

► Can we have a quieter table?

我們可以選安靜一點的位子嗎？

▶ 無法安排指定座位

問 We would like the seats near the window.

我們想要靠窗的位子。

答 I am sorry, but we don't have other seats available.

很抱歉，但是我們沒有其他空位了。

對方可以這麼說:

▶ I'm afraid that table is reserved.

那一桌恐怕有人訂了。

▶ 接受餐廳安排的座位

問 We don't have other seats available.

我們沒有其他空位了。

答 OK. Forget it.

好吧，算了。

▶ 入座

問 Please be seated, ladies and gentlemen.

請坐下，各位先生小姐。

答 Thank you so much.

感謝您。

對方可以這麼說:

▶ Please take a seat, madam.

女士，請坐。

▶ 入座後提供開水

問 Please be seated, ladies and gentlemen.

請坐下，各位先生小姐們。

答 Would you please bring me a glass of water first?

你能先幫我送一杯水來嗎？

你還可以這麼說:

▶ May I have a glass of water?

我可以要一杯水嗎？

▶ 服務生隨後來點餐

問 I will be right back for your order.

我待會馬上回來為您服務點餐。

答 Thank you.

謝謝你。

你還可以這麼說:

► Take your time. I will be right back with you.

慢慢來。我待會再來。

► A waiter will come to take your order.

服務生會來侍候您點菜。

► 要求看菜單

問 May I see the menu, please?

請給我看菜單。

答 Sure. Here you are.

好的，請看。

► 提供菜單

問 Here is your menu.

這是你們的菜單。

答 Thank you.

謝謝你。

▶ 打算慢慢看菜單

問 We will let you know if we are ready to order.
等我們準備好點餐的時候會讓你知道。

答 No problem. Take your time.
沒問題。慢慢來。

你還可以這麼說:

- We are not ready to order now.
  我們現在還沒有要點餐。
- Can we order later?
  我們可以等一下再點餐嗎？

▶ 詢問是否要開始點餐

問 May I take your order?
您要點餐了嗎？

答 Yes, I'd like a turkey sandwich.
是的，我要一個火雞三明治。

對方可以這麼說:

► Are you ready to order?

您準備好點餐了嗎？

► 開始點餐

問 Ready to order now?

準備好現在要點餐了嗎？

答 Yes, we are ready.

是的，我們準備好了。

你還可以這麼說:

► Yes, I want to order Spaghetti.

是的，我要點義大利麵。

► Yes, I'll take the "A" course.

是的，我要A餐。

► 尚未決定餐點

問 Are you ready to order?

你們準備好點餐了嗎？

答 Sorry, we have not decided yet.

對不起，我們還沒有決定。

你還可以這麼說:

► I haven't decided yet.

我還沒有決定。

► 餐廳的特餐／招牌菜

問 What is today's special?

今天的特餐是什麼？

答 It's Fillet Steak.

是菲力牛排。

你還可以這麼說:

► What's today's special to the house?

今天餐廳的特餐是什麼？

► What's the specialty?

招牌菜是什麼？

► What's the specialty of the restaurant?

餐廳的招牌菜是什麼？

▶ 請服務生推薦餐點

問 What would you recommend?

你有什麼好的推薦嗎？

答 The Italian Sea Food is the best one.

義大利海鮮食物是最棒的。

你還可以這麼說:

▶ What's your advice?

你的建議呢？

▶ What is your suggestion?

你的建議呢？

▶ 服務生徵詢推薦餐點

問 May I suggest something?

我能為您推薦一些嗎？

答 Sure.

當然好。

你還可以這麼說:

▶ Please.

請(推薦)。

▶ Please do if it's not bothering you.

請推薦如果不麻煩的話。

▶ 服務生推薦餐點

問 How about the seafood?

海鮮如何？

答 Seafood? Sounds great.

海鮮？聽起來不錯。

對方可以這麼說:

▶ Why don't you try smoked salmon?

您何不試試煙燻鮭魚？

▶ You can try our specialty of the house.

您可以試試我們的招牌菜。

▶ 對餐點的偏好

問 What kind of cuisine do you like? American or Italian?

你喜歡哪一種菜餚？美式或義式？

答 What do you have for Italian?

你們義式有那些種類？

你還可以這麼說:

▶ I have no idea for them.

我對這些不太清楚。

▶ I like French cuisine.

我喜歡法式菜。

▶ 點服務生介紹的餐點

問 You should try our sea food.

你應要試試我們的海鮮。

答 It sounds good. I will try it.

聽起來不錯，我點這一個。

你還可以這麼說:

► OK. I will try this one.

好，我要試這一種。

► I will have Sirloin Steak and salmon for the lady.

我要點沙朗牛排，小姐要鮭魚。

► 餐點售完／無供應

問 I would like to order Sirloin Steak.
我要點沙朗牛排。

答 I am sorry, but Sirloin Steak is sold out.
很抱歉，沙朗牛排賣完了。

對方可以這麼說:

► It's been sold out.

這道菜已經賣完了。

► It is not on the menu.

菜單上沒有這道菜。

► Sirloin Steak is only available on weekends.
沙朗牛排只有在週末供應。

▶ 詢問餐點配方

問 What kind of dish is it?
這是什麼菜？

答 It's American seafood marinated in lemon juice and chili peppers.
這是一美式海鮮，用檸檬汁和胡椒醃漬。

你還可以這麼說:

▶ What is the recipe?
這是什麼配方？

▶ Do you serve beefsteak pie with gravy?
你們有供應有肉汁的牛排派嗎？

▶ 服務生解釋餐點調配

問 What is the recipe?
這是什麼配方？

答 It is beef stewed in red wine.
那是用紅酒燉煮的牛肉。

對方可以這麼說:

► This dish contains pork.

這道菜有豬肉。

► It has a very rich taste.

這道菜口味很重。

► 餐點食用人數

問 I'll this course for three of us.

我要點這道餐給我們三個人。

答 I think this course will be suitable for two persons.

我覺得這道餐點兩個人食用比較適合。

► 前菜

問 What do you want for salad?

你要什麼沙拉？

答 First, I would like the vegetable salad.

首先，我要蔬菜沙拉。

你還可以這麼說:

▶ What salads do you have?

您們有什麼樣的沙拉？

▶ 介紹沙拉

問 What salads do you serve?

您們有什麼樣的沙拉？

答 We have Mixed Salad, Seafood Salad and Chef's Choice Salad.

我們有綜合沙拉、海鮮沙拉和主廚沙拉。

▶ 前菜醬料

問 Which kind of salad dressing would you prefer?

請問您要哪一種沙拉佐料？

答 French, please.

請給我法式醬料。

你還可以這麼說:

▶ I want Thousand Island.

我要千島醬。

▶ 點主菜

問 What do you want for the entrée?
您的正餐要點什麼？

答 I would like to order Sirloin Steak.
我要沙朗牛排。

對方可以這麼說:

► How about the meal?
您的正餐要點什麼？

► What would you like for your main course?
主餐您要點什麼？

▶ 服務生詢問第二位點餐者

問 How about your order, madam?
女士，您要點什麼呢？

答 I will try Roast Chicken.
我要試試烤雞。

你還可以這麼說:

► Both of us would like Fillet Steak.

我們兩個都要菲力牛排。

► I'll have a mixed Salad and a Sirloin Steak.

我要一份綜合沙拉和一客沙朗牛排。

► 點相同餐點

問 May I take your order now?

我可以幫您點餐了嗎？

答 Can I have the same as that?

我能點和那個一樣的嗎？

你還可以這麼說:

► Make it two.

點兩份。

► Same here.

我也是點相同的餐點。

► I am going to order the same thing.

我要點一樣的餐。

► I will have that, too.

我也要那個。

► We'd like this course for two, please.

這道菜請給我們來兩人份的。

► 持續點餐

問 And what would you like after that?

在這個之後您要點什麼？

答 Then I want some pizza, too.

然後我還要披薩。

對方可以這麼說:

► And then?

然後呢？

► 不供應特定餐點

問 I would like New York Steak.

我要點紐約牛排。

答 I am sorry, but we don't have New York Steak now.

很抱歉，但是我們現在沒有紐約牛排。

▶ 牛排烹調的熟度

問 How do you like your steak cooked?

您的牛排要幾分熟？

答 Well done, please.

請給我全熟。

你還可以這麼說:

▶ Medium, please.

請給我五分熟。

▶ Medium rare, please.

請給我四分熟。

▶ Rare, please.

請給我三分熟。

▶ 副餐

問 Which vegetables come with the steak?

牛排的副菜是什麼？

答 Onion rings and noodles.

洋蔥圈和麵。

對方可以這麼說:

▶ This dish contains fried eggs and vegetables.

這道餐有煎蛋和蔬菜。

▶ There are several side dishes.

有許多種副餐。

▶ 湯點

問 We have both clear soup and thick soup.

我們有清湯和濃湯都有。

答 I want to try seafood soup.

我要試一試海鮮湯。

你還可以這麼說:

▶ I would like a cup of onion soup.

我要洋蔥湯。

▶ 詢問麵種類

問 What kind of bread do you want?

您要哪一種麵包?

答 What do you have?

你們有那些?

你還可以這麼說:

► What do you serve?

你們有供應哪些？

► 甜點介紹

問 Which flavor would you prefer, walnut or vanilla?

您喜歡哪一種口味的，核桃還是香草？

答 Vanilla is my favorite.

香草是我最喜歡的。

► 要求再提供甜點

問 And would you bring us some bread?

你能再給我們一些麵包嗎？

答 Yes, I will be right back.

好的，我馬上回來。

你還可以這麼說:

► I want some too, please.

我也要一些。

► Please give me another sandwich.

請再給我另一份三明治。

► 詢問甜點種類

問 How about the dessert?
點心呢？

答 I want pudding.
我要布丁。

對方可以這麼說:

► After the meal, what would you like for dessert?

正餐後，你要什麼甜點？

► 點甜點

問 After the meal, what would you like for dessert?
正餐後，你要什麼甜點？

答 I want some cookies, please.
我要一些餅乾。

你還可以這麼說:

▶ I will try ice cream.
我要點冰淇淋。

▶ I want to have chocolate cake.
我要吃巧克力蛋糕。

▶ I would like cheese cake.
我要點起司蛋糕。

▶ 詢問是否要點飲料

問 Would you like something to drink?
你要不要來點飲料？

答 I want something cold.
我想要喝點冷飲。

對方可以這麼說:

▶ Anything to drink?
飲料呢？

▶ Which would you prefer, tea or coffee?
您要茶還是咖啡？

► Would you like to order some wine with your meal?

您想不想叫點酒配食物？

► 點酒類飲料

問 What kind of alcohol do you want?

您要喝什麼酒？

答 I would like the brandy.

我要白蘭地酒。

你還可以這麼說:

► Brandy, please.

請給我白蘭地。

► Beer is fine.

啤酒就好。

► 請服務生推薦飲料

問 What is your suggestion for drinks?

你對飲料的建議是什麼？

答 We have, brandy and beer.

我們有白蘭地和啤酒。

▶ 點飲料

問 Would you like to have a cup of rose tea? It's very popular.

喝杯玫瑰茶怎麼樣？這個很受歡迎。

答 It sounds terrific. I will take it.

聽起來很棒。我就點這個。

你還可以這麼說:

▶ Interesting. I will take it.

很有趣。我點這一種。

▶ Coffee would be fine.

就點咖啡。

▶ Coke, please.

請給我可樂。

▶ 要求再提供飲料

問 May I have some more wine, please?

我能再多要一些酒嗎？

答 OK. I will be right back with you.

是的，我馬上回來。

對方可以這麼說:

▶ Now or later?

現在要還是待會要？

▶ 詢問是否完成點餐

問 Both of us would like Sirloin Steak.
我們兩個都要沙朗牛排。

答 Two Sirloin Steak. Is that all?
兩份沙朗牛排。就這樣嗎？

對方可以這麼說:

▶ Is that all for order?

您點的就這些嗎？

▶ Anything else?

還有沒有要其他餐點？

▶ 是否要點其他餐點

問 What else are you going to have?
您還要點什麼嗎？

答 I think it's enough now.

我想這就夠了。

對方可以這麼說:

- Anything else?

還有沒有要其他餐點?

- Will that be all?

就這樣?

- Is there anything else?

還要不要別的?

▶ 提供咖啡的時間

問 When would you like your coffee? Now or later?

您什麼時候要上咖啡?現在或稍後?

答 Later, please.

請稍後再上。

你還可以這麼說:

- Right now, please.

現在就給我。

▶ Mine is now, but hers is after the meal.

我的現在上，她的用完餐後上。

▶ 確認已點完餐點

問 Is that all?

就這樣嗎？

答 That's all for us.

就這樣了。

你還可以這麼說:

▶ Yes. That's it.

是的，就這些。

▶ That's all, thanks.

就這樣，謝謝。

▶ 服務生完成餐點

問 OK. The meal will be served soon.

好的，餐點會盡快為您送上。

答 Thanks.

謝謝！

▶ 催促盡快上菜

問 Could you serve us as soon as possible?

你能不能盡快為我們上菜？

答 No problem.

沒問題。

你還可以這麼說:

▶ Could you serve us quickly?

你能不能快一點為我們上菜？

▶ I ordered my meal forty minutes ago and it still hasn't come.

我至少在四十分鐘前點的菜，到現在還沒有來。

▶ Why is my steak taking so long?

為什麼我的牛排要這麼久？

▶ 請同桌者遞調味料

問 Excuse me, please pass me the salt.

對不起，請遞給我鹽。

答 Sure, here you are.
當然好，給你。

▶ 服務生詢問是否可以上菜

問 May I serve your meal now?
現在可以上您的餐點嗎？

答 Yes, please.
好的，請便。

對方可以這麼說:

- May I serve your soup now?
  現在可以上湯點嗎？
- May I serve coffee now?
  現在可以上咖啡嗎？
- May I serve it to you now?
  我現在可以幫您上菜了嗎？

▶ 上菜

問 This dish is very hot. Please be careful.
這道菜很燙，請小心。

答 Thanks.

謝謝。

對方可以這麼說:

► Enjoy your meal.

請好好享用。

► This dish is best eaten while hot.

這道餐點最好趁熱吃。

► Please have them with this sauce.

請沾這個醬料食用。

► 服務生上菜時確認點餐者

問 You ordered the beef sandwich, right?

您點牛肉三明治，對吧？

答 No. That's hers.

不是。那是她點的。

對方可以這麼說:

► Is this yours?

這是您點的嗎？

► Your Sirloin Steak, sir.

先生，您的沙朗牛排要上菜了。

▶ 上菜時說明自己的餐點

問 Who has the onion rings?

誰點洋蔥圈？

答 They are ours. We are sharing them.

他們是我們（點）的。我們要一起吃。

▶ 自行分配點餐

問 Whose order?

誰點的餐？

答 Why don't you just put everything down on the table?

你要不要就放在桌上就好？

你 還可以這麼說:

▶ We will figure it out.

我們自己會處理。

▶ 送錯餐點

問 This is not what I ordered.

這不是我點的餐點。

答 Sorry, sir. I will check your order right now.

抱歉，先生。我馬上查您的餐點。

對方可以這麼說:

▶ I'm very sorry, sir. What was your order?

先生真對不起，您點的是什麼？

▶ I'm very sorry for the mistake.

抱歉弄錯了。

▶ I'll check your order with our Chef.

我會和主廚核對您點的菜。

▶ Sorry, sir. I'll return this steak to the Chef.

非常抱歉，先生，我會把牛排退回給主廚。

▶ 少送餐點

問 Is there a dish missing?

是不是少送一道餐點？

答 Let me check your order.

讓我查一查您的菜單。

你還可以這麼說:

► I am afraid there is a dish missing.

恐怕有一道餐點沒來。

► Where is my onion rings?

我的洋蔥圈呢？

► 主餐醬料

問 What would you like for the dressing?
您要哪一種醬料？

答 Black pepper, please.
請給我黑胡椒。

你還可以這麼說:

► I'll take both kinds of steak dressing.

兩種牛排醬料我都要。

► 侍者斟酒時

問 Say when, please.
請說夠了。

答 When.
夠了。

▶ 喝濃／淡茶

問 Do you take your tea strong or weak?
你喝濃茶還是淡茶呢？

答 Strong, please.
請給我濃的。

你 還可以這麼說:

▶ I would like my tea sweet.
我喝茶喜歡放糖。

▶ 加奶精

問 Do you take it with milk?
你喝茶要不要加牛奶？

答 No, I don't take milk with my tea.
不用，我喝茶不加牛奶。

▶ 加糖／不加糖

問 How many lumps of sugar?
要幾塊糖？

答 Two, please.
請給我兩塊。

你還可以這麼說:

► I don't drop sugar into coffee.
我喝咖啡不加糖。

► 咖啡續杯

問 May I have another cup, please?
可以再給我一杯嗎？

答 Of course, sir.
當然可以，先生。

你還可以這麼說:

► May I have a refill?
我可以續杯嗎？

► Excuse me. May I have some more coffee?
抱歉，我能多要一些咖啡嗎？

▶ 服務生詢問是否需要協助

問 Can I get you anything else?
需要我幫你們拿些其他東西嗎？

答 Well, could you bring us a few napkins?
嗯，你可以給我們一些紙巾嗎？

對方可以這麼說:

▶ Do you need anything else?
還需要其他東西嗎？

▶ 呼叫服務生

問 Excuse me.
抱歉。

答 Yes, sir, may I help you?
是的，先生，需要我的協助嗎？

你還可以這麼說:

▶ Waiter/waitress.
男/女服務生。

▶ 要求提供醬料

問 Do you have any ketchup? I think this bottle is empty.

你們有蕃茄醬嗎？我猜這一瓶的是空的。

答 Yes, we do. I will bring some right away.

有的，我們有。我馬上拿一些過來。

▶ 請服務生提供新餐具

問 I drop my fork. May I have a new one?

我的叉子掉到地上了，我能要一支新的嗎？

答 I'll change a new one for you.

我會幫您換支新的。

你還可以這麼說:

▶ This spoon is a little dirty.

這支湯匙有一點髒。

▶ I dropped my spoon on the floor.

我的湯匙掉在地上。

▶ This glass is cracked!

這個玻璃杯有裂痕！

▶ My plate is chipped!

我的盤子有缺口！

▶ 整理桌面

問 Would you clear the table for us?

你可以為我們整理一下桌子嗎？

答 Sure.

好的。

對方可以這麼說:

▶ Would you wait for a second?

您可以稍等一下嗎？

▶ Sure. I will be right back.

好的。我馬上回來。

▶ 詢問是否繼續用餐

問 Have you finished or still working on it?

您用完餐還是要繼續用？

1 答 We have finished it.

3 我們用完了。

4

對方可以這麼說:

▶ Have you finished your meal, sir?

先生，您用完餐了嗎？

▶ 尚在用餐

問 May I clear your table?
需要我幫您清理桌面嗎？

答 Leave that left.
那個留下來。

你還可以這麼說:

▶ I am still working on it.

我還在用。

▶ 取走餐盤

問 Excuse me, may I take your plate?
抱歉，我可以收走您的盤子了嗎？

答 Please. Thank you.
麻煩您，謝謝。

你還可以這麼說:

► Sure, go ahead.

好的，請便。

► 指引方向

問 Would you tell me where the lady's room is?

你能告訴我女士盥洗室在哪裡嗎？

答 This way, please.

請這裡走。

對方可以這麼說:

► Go straight along the hallway and turn right at the end.

沿著走廊直走，到盡頭右轉。

► It's right over there.

就在那個方向。

► 向服務生尋求協助

問 There's no ashtray on the table!

桌上沒有菸灰缸！

答 Yes, sir.

好的，先生。

你還可以這麼說:

▶ May I have more napkins?

能給我多一點紙巾嗎？

▶ Can you bring me the ketchup/mustard/pepper?

請拿蕃茄醬/芥末/胡椒粉來好嗎？

▶ Would you bring us a high chair for her?

可以幫我拿一張兒童椅給她嗎？

▶ Can we have another chair?

我們能再要一張椅子嗎？

▶ 向餐廳抱怨餐點

➪ This food tastes strange.

這道菜嚐起來味道很怪！

➪ The milk is sour.

牛奶發酸了。

➪ It's too oily.

太油膩了。

➪ This is tough.
（肉質）好硬啊！

➪ The meat is overdone.
肉煮過頭了。

➪ This toast is too dark!
吐司烤得太焦了！

➪ My steak is too rare.
我的牛排太生了。

➪ There's an insect in my salad!
我的沙拉裏有蟲！

➪ There is a hair in my soup!
我的湯裏有根頭髮！

➪ Can you take it back and cook it longer?
請拿回去再烤久一點好嗎？

➪ The food is getting cold.
食物變涼了。

▶ 向餐廳抱怨服務、環境

➪ We deserve better service.
我們應該享有更好的服務。

➪ The service was very bad.
服務很差。

➪ It's too noisy here.
這裡太吵了。

➪ It's very freezing/hot.
這裏面好冷/熱。

▶ 結帳

問 Bill, please.
買單。

答 Cash or credit cards?
用現金還是信用卡(付帳)?

你 還可以這麼說:

► Check, please.
請結帳。

▶ 詢問結帳方式

問 Cash or credit cards?
用現金還是信用卡(付帳)?

答 Credit cards.
信用卡(付帳)。

對方可以這麼說:

► Would you pay it by cash or credit cards?
您要用現金還是信用卡付帳?

► 說明付款方式

問 Would you pay it by cash or credit cards?
您要用現金還是信用卡付帳?

答 I will pay it by credit card.
我要用信用卡結帳。

你還可以這麼說:

► Credit cards. Here is my card.
信用卡。這是我的信用卡。

► Here is mine.
這是我的(信用卡)。

► I will pay it by cash. Here you are.
我要用現金付錢。錢給你。

▶ 分開結帳

問 Do you want separate checks?
你們要不要分開付帳？

答 OK.
好的。

對方可以這麼說:

▶ Would you like to separate your checks?
您要分開您的帳單嗎？

▶ 請客

➪ It's my treat this time.
這次我請客。

➪ I will treat you.
我請客。

➪ It's on me.
帳算我的。

➪ I insist on paying the bill.
我堅持付帳。

▶ 各付各的帳單

問 Let's go Dutch.
讓我們各付各的吧！

答 Good idea.
好主意。

▶ 帳單金額

問 It's seven hundred and seventy dollars.
總共七百七十元。

答 OK.
好。

▶ 內含服務費

問 Is the service charge included?
有包含服務費嗎？

答 Yes. It's included 10 % service charge.
是的，包含百分之十的服務費。

你還可以這麼說:

► Is this icluding service charge?

有含服務費嗎？

► 找零錢

問 Here is 100 dollars.

這是一百元。

答 Here is your receipt and change.

這是您的收據和零錢。

► 不必找零

問 Keep the change.

不用找零錢了。

答 Thank you, sir.

先生，謝謝您。

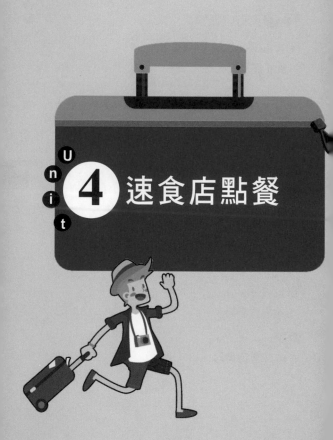

Unit 4 速食店點餐

▶ 點餐

問 I would like McChicken Nuggets.
我要點麥克雞塊。

答 Here is your order.
這是您的餐點。

你還可以這麼說:

- I'll have a Big Mac.
  我要一個麥香堡。
- I'll have a small fries.
  我要一份小薯條。
- I'll have a hamburger with a lot of ketchup.
  我要點一個大漢堡，要有很多蕃茄醬。

▶ 選擇內用或外帶

問 Stay or to go?
要這裏用還是外帶？

答 Stay, please.
內用，麻煩你。

你還可以這麼說:

▶ That'll be for here.

要在這裡吃。

▶ To go, please.

帶走，麻煩你。

▶ 餐點售完／無供應

問 A chicken sandwich to go, please.
我要外帶一份雞肉三明治。

答 It is sold out.
賣完了。

對方可以這麼說:

▶ It's been sold out.

它已經賣完了。

▶ 等待外帶餐點

問 Then I want the beef sandwich and an apple pie.
那麼我要牛肉三明治和蘋果派。

答 Wait a moment, please.
請稍候。

對方可以這麼說:

► You'll have to wait for 10 minutes.
您要等十分鐘喔！

► 要求加快餐點外帶速度

問 Could you make it quickly? I have to catch the train.
你能快一點嗎？我要去趕火車。

答 Yes, sir.
好的，先生。

► 醬料的種類

問 What sauces would you like?
你要什麼醬料？

答 Ketchup, please.
請給我蕃茄醬。

你還可以這麼說:

► Make it strawberry.

要草莓口味的。

► I want two hamburgers, one plain, the other with all trimmings to go.

我要外帶兩個漢堡，一個什麼都不加，另一個全部的佐料都要。

► 添加醬料

問 Would you like anything on it?

你要加什麼在上面嗎？

答 Yes, cheese and a lot of mustard.

好的，要起司和很多芥末。

你還可以這麼說:

► Butter, please.

請給我奶油。

► Make it honey.

要蜂蜜口味的。

► No, thanks.

不用，謝謝。

▶ 多要一些醬料

問 Can I have extra ketchup?
我能多要一份蕃茄醬嗎？

答 Sure. Here you are.
當然，這是您要的。

▶ 飲料

問 Do you want any drinks?
您要點飲料嗎？

答 I want Coke.
我要可樂。

你 還可以這麼說:

▶ I'd like a milk shake.

我要一杯奶昔。

▶ 說明飲料大小杯

問 Large?
大杯嗎？

答 Yes, a large root beer.
要，來一杯大杯沙士。

你還可以這麼說:

► I want medium, not large.
我要中杯，不是大杯。

► Regular, please.
(請給我)普通杯。

► And a large Coke, please.
還要一杯大杯可口可樂。

► 詢問是否需要糖包或奶精

問 I would like a cup of coffee, please.
請給我一杯咖啡。

答 Cream or sugar?
要奶精還是糖？

對方可以這麼說:

► Would you like cream or sugar?
您要奶精還是糖？

▶ How do you like your coffee?

咖啡要多少奶精和糖？

▶ 糖包和奶精都要

問 Would you like cream or sugar?
您要奶精還是糖？

答 I would like both, thank you.
我兩種都要，謝謝。

你還可以這麼說:

▶ Both.

兩個都要。

▶ 說明糖包和奶精的量

問 How about you, sir?
先生，您呢？

答 Coffee, two sugars and two cream, please
請給我咖啡、兩包糖和兩包奶精。

你還可以這麼說:

► Two sugars and no cream.

糖兩包，不要奶精。

► Just cream, please.

只要奶精。

► 索取紙巾、吸管

問 Can I have more napkins?
我可以多要一些紙巾嗎？

答 Here you are.
在這裡。

你還可以這麼說:

► May I have more straws?

我可以多要一些吸管嗎？

English For Travel

Unit 5 購物

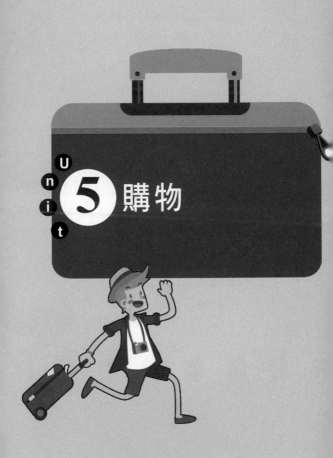

▶ 詢問營業時間

問 How late are you open?
你們營業到幾點？

答 Until six thirty.
到六點卅分。

對方可以這麼說:

- We are open until six thirty.
  我們營業到六點卅分。
- We are open all night.
  我們整晚都有營業。
- We are open from 11 am to 9 pm.
  我們從早上十一點營業到晚上九點。
- On Saturday we are open from 9 am to 7 pm.
  星期六我們營業從早上九點到晚上七點。

▶ 只看不買

問 May I help you with something?
需要我幫忙的嗎？

答 No. I am just looking.
不用。我只是隨便看看。

你還可以這麼說:

▶ No. Thanks.

不用，謝謝！

▶ Maybe later. Thank you.

也許等一下要（麻煩您），謝謝。

▶ I don't need any help.

我不需要你服務。

▶ Not yet. Thanks.

還不需要。謝謝！

▶ 店員主動招呼

問 Hi, are you being helped?
嗨，有人為您服務嗎？

答 No. I'm interested in those gloves.
沒有。我對那一些手套有興趣。

你還可以這麼說:

▶ No. I am just looking.

沒有。我隨便看看。

▶ Yes. I am waiting for David.

有的，我正在等大衛。

▶ 店員的客套話

問 I am just looking.

我隨便看看。

答 If you need any help, just let me know. My name is David.

假如您需要任何幫忙，讓我知道就好，我是大衛。

對方可以這麼說:

▶ Take your time.

您慢慢看。

▶ 購物的打算

問 I am looking for some gifts for my kids.

我在找一些要送給孩子們的禮物。

答 Is there anything special in mind?

心裡有想好要什麼嗎？

你還可以這麼說:

► Is there any souvenirs made in the USA?

有沒有美國製造的紀念品？

► I need to buy birthday presents for my wife.

我需要幫我太太買生日禮物。

► 購買特定商品

問 What do you want to buy?

您想買什麼？

答 I want to buy the earings.

我想要買耳環。

你還可以這麼說:

► I need a pair of gloves.

我需要手套。

► I am looking for some skirts.

我正在找一些裙子。

► Do you have any purple hats?

你們有紫色的帽子嗎？

▶ 購買禮品

問 Is it a present for someone?
送給誰的禮物嗎？

答 Yes, it's for my daughter.
是的，是給我女兒的。

對方可以這麼說:

▶ Looking for anything special?
要找特定的東西嗎？

▶ They are suitable presents for family.
他們是很適合送家人的禮物。

▶ 購買電器

問 Does it have a warranty?
這個有保證書嗎？

答 Yes, it does, sir.
有的，先生。

▶ 參觀特定商品

問 What would you like to see?
您想看些什麼？

答 I would like to see some ties.
我想看一些領帶。

你還可以這麼說:

- May I see those MP3 players?
  我能看那些MP3播放器嗎？
- May I have a look at them?
  我能看一看他們嗎？
- Can you show me something different?
  你能給我看一些不一樣的嗎？
- Show me that pen.
  給我看那支筆。

▶ 詢問是否找到中意商品

問 Did you find something you like?
找到您喜歡的東西了嗎？

答 Yes, I am interested in this computer.
對，我對這台電腦有興趣。

你還可以這麼說:

► Not yet.
還沒有。

► It looks nice.
這個看起來不錯。

► Do you have any hats like this one?
你們有沒有像這類的帽子？

► 選購指定商品

問 Which one do you like?
你喜歡哪一件？

答 Please show me that black sweater.
請給我看看那件黑色毛衣。

你還可以這麼說:

► That one on the bottom shelf.
在底層架子上的那一件。

► Those skirts look great.
那些裙子看起來不錯。

▶ 回答是否尋找特定商品

問 Is this what you are looking for?
你要找的是這一種嗎？

答 Yes, I want this one.
是的，我要這一種。

你還可以這麼說:

▶ No, I don't like this one.
不要，我不喜歡這一件。

▶ Anything else?
還有其他嗎？

▶ Do you have anything better?
你有沒有好一點的？

▶ Is that all?
全部就這些嗎？

▶ 回答是否選購指定商品

問 Do you need a pair of pants?
您需要褲子嗎？

答 Yes, I want to take a look.
是的，我想要看一看。

你 還可以這麼說:

► No, thanks.

不用，謝謝！

► It's not what I need.

這不是我需要的。

► It's not what I am looking for.

我不是要找這一種。

► 詢問特殊商品

問 We have some nice ones on sale.
我們有一些品質不錯在特價中。

答 Where are they?
在哪裡？

你 還可以這麼說:

► What are they?

是什麼？

▶ What's the discount?

折扣是多少？

▶ Would you show me something special?

可以給我看一些特別的嗎？

▶ 推薦商品

問 Maybe you would like a wool scarf.

也許您想要一條羊毛圍巾。

答 Yes, I think that's what I want.

對，我想這就是我要的。

你還可以這麼說:

▶ No, it's too heavy.

不要，這個太重了。

▶ I don't think my wife would like it.

我不這麼認為我太太會喜歡。

▶ 新品上市

問 They are new arrivals.

他們都是新品。

答 Can I pick it up?
我可以看看嗎？

你還可以這麼說:

► Is it expensive?

貴嗎？

► No discount for new arrivals?

新品沒有折扣嗎？

► 商品的操作

問 Woukld you show me how it works?
你可以操作給我看嗎？

答 Sure, sir. You can push this button to turn it on.
好的，先生。你可以按這個鈕來開啟電源。

你還可以這麼說:

► How to use this?

這個要怎麼用？

► How do I operate it?

要怎麼操作？

▶ 特定顏色

問 What color do you like?
您想要哪一個顏色？

答 Do you have any ones in blue?
你們有藍色的嗎？

你還可以這麼說:

▶ I am looking for a pair of blues socks.
我在找藍色的襪子。

▶ Both red and blue are OK.
紅色或藍色都可以。

▶ Do you have this size in any other colors?
有這個尺寸的其他顏色嗎？

▶ 選擇顏色

問 I prefer blue.
我喜歡藍色。

答 OK. Let me take some blue skirts for you.
好的，讓我拿一些藍色裙子給您。

對方可以這麼說:

▶ We only have red ones.

先生，我們只有紅色。

▶ We are out of blue, sir.

先生，我們沒有藍色。

▶ Would you like to see black ones?

您要看看黑色的嗎？

▶ Let me look in the stockroom.

讓我到倉庫確定一下。

▶ 特定款式

問 What style would you like?

您想要哪一種款式？

答 More fashionable.

流行一點的。

你還可以這麼說:

▶ That's the style this year, isn't it?

這是今年的款式，對吧？

▶ Do you have plain ones?

有沒有樸素一點的？

► I prefer conservative ones.

我偏好保守一點的。

► 款式的差異

問 What is the difference between the model A and B?

款式A和款式B有什麼不同？

答 The model A is new arrival.

款式A是新貨。

你還可以這麼說:

► What is the difference between them?

他們兩個有什麼不同？

► I can't tell the difference.

我看不出來有什麼差別。

► Is this one different from that red one?

這個和紅色那個不同嗎？

► 特定搭配

問 What dose it go with?

什麼會和這一件搭配？

答 This sweater goes with them.
這件毛衣和他們可以搭配穿。

你還可以這麼說:

► This jacket will match those pants nicely.
這件夾克和那條褲子會十分相配。

► Both red and black match it.
紅色和黑色都和它很配。

► They look great together.
他們配起來不錯。

► 流行款式

問 Which one is better?
哪一件比較好？

答 Red is in fashion.
紅色正在流行。

對方可以這麼說:

► This is now in fashion.
這種現在正流行。

► Loose pants are very fashionable.
寬鬆的褲子非常流行。

▶ 尺寸說明

問 What is your size?
您的尺寸是多少？

答 My size is 8.
我的尺寸是八號。

你還可以這麼說:

▶ I don't know my size.
我知道我的尺寸。

▶ My size is between 8 and 7.
我的尺寸是介於八號和七號之間。

▶ 特定尺寸

問 What size do you want?
您要什麼尺寸？

答 Medium, please.
請給我中號。

你還可以這麼說:

► I want the large size.

我要大尺寸的。

► I will try on a small.

我要試穿小號的。

► It's a small and I wear a medium.

這是小號的，我穿中號的。

► 詢問尺寸

問 Any other sizes?
有沒有其他尺寸？

答 This comes in several sizes.
這有好多種尺寸。

你還可以這麼說:

► What sizes do you have?

你們有什麼尺寸？

► Do you have this one in small size?

你們有小號的嗎？

► Give me size 8.

給我八號。

► Size 8 in black.

給我黑色的八號尺寸。

► 不知道尺寸

問 I don't know what my size is.
我不知道我的尺寸。

答 I can measure you up.
我可以幫你量。

對方可以這麼說:

► It's size 32, right?

是三十二號，對嗎？

► Your size is 8, I guess.

我猜你的尺寸是八號。

► Let me measure your waist.

我幫你量腰圍。

► I can measure you for your suit.

我可以幫你量西裝。

▶ 不中意商品

問 What do you think of those?

那些你覺得呢？

答 It seems a little old-fashioned.

好像有些老氣。

你還可以這麼說:

▶ It's not the right size.

尺寸不對。

▶ I don't this style.

我不喜歡這個款式。

▶ I don't prefer this kind of color.

我不偏好這種顏色。

▶ 回答試穿與否

問 Would you like to try it on?

你要試穿看看嗎？

答 OK.

好。

你還可以這麼說:

▶ No, thanks.

不用了，謝謝。

▶ 要求試穿

問 Can I try this on?

我可以試穿這一件嗎？

答 Sure. This way please.

好啊，這邊請。

對方可以這麼說:

▶ Sure. Here you are.

好的。這是你要的。

▶ Sure. You can try this one.

當然好。您可以試穿這一件。

▶ Fitting room is over there.

試衣間在那裡。

▶ I am sorry, but it's not allowed to try it on.

抱歉，不可以試穿。

▶ 提供試穿

問 Try this coat on and see if it fits.
試穿這件外套，看看是否合身。

答 Thanks.
謝謝。

你還可以這麼說:

- Where is the fitting room?
  試穿間在哪裡？
- May I try on that one, too?
  我也可以試穿那一件嗎？
- No, thanks.
  不用，謝謝！

▶ 試穿特定尺寸

問 How about this size?
這一個尺寸如何？

答 I should try another bigger one.
我應該要試穿另一件大一點的。

你還可以這麼說:

▶ Could I try a larger one?

可以換大一點的嗎？

▶ Can I try a smaller one?

我能試穿較小件的嗎？

▶ Do you have this color in size 38?

這個顏色有三十八號嗎？

▶ Do you have these shoes in size 7?

您有七號的鞋子嗎？

▶ 徵詢試穿尺寸

問 Would you like to try a larger size?

您要試穿大一點的嗎？

答 Yes, please.

好的，請給我。

你還可以這麼說:

▶ Yes, I will try on size 42.

好的，我要試穿四十二號。

▶ No, this size is fine.

不用，這個尺寸可以。

▶ 詢問試穿結果

問 How does this one look on me?
我穿這一件的效果怎麼樣？

答 It looks great on you.
你穿看起來不錯。

你 還可以這麼說:

▶ Where is the mirror?

鏡子那裡？

▶ Take a look for me.

幫我看一看。

▶ 質疑試穿結果

問 It looks good on you.
你穿這件看起來不錯耶！

答 I don't think so.
我不這麼認為。

你還可以這麼說:

▶ You think so?

你這麼認為嗎？

▶ I have no idea.

我拿不定主意。

▶ I don't think this is good.

我不覺得這件好。

▶ Don't you think it's too loose?

你不覺得太寬鬆嗎？

▶ 試穿結果不錯

問 How do they feel?
他們覺得如何？

答 It feels fine.
我覺得不錯。

你還可以這麼說:

▶ It's great.

好看。

▶ Not bad.

不錯。

▶ It looks perfect to me.

這個我喜歡。

▶ It looks OK on me.

我穿看起來不錯。

▶ 特定尺寸不適合

問 Does it fit?

合身嗎？

答 Well, the waist was a little tight.

嗯，腰部有一點緊。

你還可以這麼說:

▶ It really feels tight.

真的有一些緊。

▶ The legs weren't long enough.

褲腳的長度不夠。

▶ They were just too small.

他們太小了。

▶ They seem a little big.

好像有一些大。

▶ 試穿結果不喜歡

問 Your clothes fit perfectly.
你的衣服十分合身。

答 But it's not very comfortable.
但是(穿起來)不舒服。

你還可以這麼說:

▶ Something wrong with this one.
這件不太對勁。

▶ It makes me look fat.
這個讓我看起來很胖。

▶ It's not I expect.
和我預期的不同。

▶ 說明試穿特定尺寸

問 What do you think of size 36?
你覺得三十六號呢？

答 It's too tight.
太緊了。

你還可以這麼說:

► It feels tight.

我覺得緊。

► It was too small.

這件太小了。

► They were too big.

它們太大了。

► This is too loose for me.

這件對我來說太鬆了。

► 沒有庫存

問 Do you have this shirt in size 38?
這件襯衫有沒有三十八號？

答 Yes, let me take one for you.
有的，讓我拿一件給您。

對方可以這麼說:

► If you can't find them on the rack, they may be out of stock.

假如架上沒有發現，也許就沒有庫存了。

▶ Yes. What color do you prefer? Black or brown?

有的。您要哪一種顏色？黑色或棕色？

▶ I am not sure. Let me take a look.

我不確定。讓我看一看。

▶ 說明是否喜歡

問 How do you like it?
你喜歡嗎？

答 I like this one.
我喜歡這一件。

你還可以這麼說:

▶ I don't like them.

我不喜歡它們。

▶ Let me think about it for a second.

我想一想。

▶ I don't know.

我不知道。

▶ 要求提供其他樣式

問 Is that all you have?
你們只有這些？

答 This comes in many colors.
這有許許多種顏色。

對方可以這麼說:

▶ That's all we have.
這是我們所有的了。

▶ Which brand do you want?
您想要哪一個牌子？

▶ What style would you like to see?
您想看什麼款式？

▶ How about these ones?
這一些如何？

▶ 回答是否參觀其他商品

問 Can I show you anything else?
需要我給您看一些其他商品嗎？

答 Yes, please.
好啊。

你還可以這麼說:

- Any other colors?

  有沒有其他顏色？
- Any other styles?

  有沒有其他款式？
- No, that's enough.

  不用，夠了。

▶ 特價期限

問 This promotion ends tomorrow.
這個優惠明天就結束了。

答 But I have to think about it.
但是我要考慮一下。

對方可以這麼說:

- Our sale will be continuing until next week.

  我們的特價只到下週。

▶ 說服購買

問 It's a very good buy.
很划算的。

答 OK, I will take them.
好，我買。

對方可以這麼說:

- It's a bargain.
這很划算的。
- It's very cheap.
它很便宜。
- It's worth.
很值得。

▶ 詢問售價

問 You know, that sweater's a great buy.
你知道嗎，這件毛衣真的很划算。

答 How much?
多少錢？

你還可以這麼說:

► How much is this?

這個要多少錢。

► How much does it cost?

這個要賣多少錢？

► How much did you say?

你說要多少錢？

► What is the price?

價錢是多少？

► 詢問特定商品的售價

問 What's the price for this camera?
這台相機多少錢？

答 Two thousand.
兩千元。

對方可以這麼說:

► It's two thousand dollars.

賣兩千元。

▶ 購買二件以上的價格

問 How much is it together?
總共多少錢？

答 It's only $250.
只要二百五十元。

你還可以這麼說:

- How much shall I pay for them?
  我應該付多少錢？
- How much shall I pay for this one and that one?
  這一件和那一件我應該付多少錢？
- Can you lower the price a bit if I buy them?
  如果我買他們，你可以算便宜一點嗎？

▶ 含稅價

問 It costs seven hundred dollars plus tax.
它含稅要七千元。

答 So expensive?
這麼貴？

你還可以這麼說：

► I can't afford it.
我付不起。

► 購物幣值

問 Can I buy it in New Taiwan dollars?
我可以用新台幣買嗎？

答 I am afrain not, sir.
恐怕不行，先生。

對方可以這麼說：

► Yes. We accept New Taiwan dollars.
可以的。我們接受台幣。

► 討價還價

問 What do you think of the price?
你覺得價格如何？

答 It's too expensive.
它太貴了。

你還可以這麼說:

▶ Do you think it's possible to get a discount?
你認為可以給我個折扣嗎？

▶ Are there any discounts?
有沒有折扣？

▶ Can you give me a discount?
你可以給我折扣嗎？

▶ Can you make it cheaper?
可以算便宜一點嗎？

▶ 特定價格的討價還價

問 Can you lower the price?
可以算便宜一點的嗎？

答 What price range are you looking for?
你想要多少錢？

你還可以這麼說:

► Can you lower it two hundred?

可以便宜兩百元嗎？

► Can you give me a 10 percent discount?

你能給我九折嗎？

► How about five thousand dollars?

可以算五千元嗎？

► 購買多件的討價還價

問 Can you give me a discount if I buy two sweaters?

如果我買兩件毛衣，你可以給我折扣嗎？

答 But you have to pay it by cash.

可是你要付現金。

你還可以這麼說:

► Is there a discount for two?

買兩件可以有折扣吧？

▶ 最後底線的報價

問 Are there any discounts?
沒有折扣？

答 How about a 10 percent discount? That's the best I can offer.
打九折如何？這是我能提供最優惠的價格了。

對方可以這麼說:

▶ I am afraid not.
恐怕不行。

▶ What price range do you want?
你心裡預算多少錢？

▶ 決定購買

問 Would you like to buy it?
您要買嗎？

答 I will buy this one.
我要買這一件。

你還可以這麼說:

► I will take it.

我要買這一件。

► I will get this one.

我要買這一件。

► I want both of them.

我兩件都要。

► I will two of these.

我要買這兩件。

► 不考慮購買

問 Would you like to buy it?

您要買嗎？

答 No, I will pass this time.

不要，我這次不買。

你還可以這麼說:

► Not for this time.

這次先不要（買）。

▶ 付款方式

問 How would you like to pay for it?
您要用什麼方式付款？

答 Cash, please.
用現金。

你 還可以這麼說:

▶ Credit card, please.
我要用信用卡付款。

▶ I will pay it by cash.
我要付現。

▶ With traveler's check.
用旅行支票(付款)。

▶ 付款方式

問 Do you accept credit cards?
你們接受信用卡付款嗎？

答 Yes, we do.
是的，我們有。

答 Sorry, we only accept cash.
抱歉，我們只收現金。

你還可以這麼說:

► Can I use VISA?

我可以用VISA卡嗎？

► Do you take Master?

你們接受萬事達卡嗎？

► 要求包裝

問 Could you wrap it up for me?

你能幫我打包嗎？

答 OK. Would you wait for a second?

好的。能請您稍等一下嗎？

你還可以這麼說:

► Would you wrap it as a present?

可以包裝成禮物嗎？

► Would you put them in a box?

可以把他們放進盒子裡嗎？

▶ 禮品包裝

問 Could you gift-wrap it?
你能幫我打包成禮品嗎？

答 Certainly, sir.
當然可以，先生。

對方可以這麼說:

▶ I am sorry, sir, but we don't have this service.
抱歉，先生，但是我們沒有這項服務。

▶ 其他相關問題

➪ Do you have free tailoring?
你們有免費修改嗎？

➪ Could you adjust the pants length?
你能修改褲子長度嗎？

➪ Could I return it if I don't like it?
如果我不喜歡能退還嗎？

➪ Can you give me a receipt?
可以給我收據嗎？

➩ You don't give me the right change.
你沒找對錢。

➩ This camera is defective. Can I have it replaced?
這台相機有問題。我可以換一台嗎？

➩ I would like to return it. This is the receipt.
我想要退貨。這是收據。

➩ May I exchange it for another brand?
我可以換另一個牌子嗎？

➩ Can I get a refund for it?
我能退錢嗎？

English For Travel

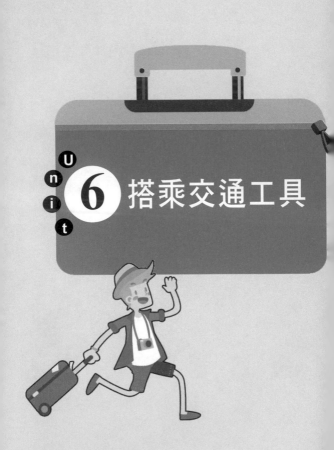

Unit 6 搭乘交通工具

▶ 計程車招呼站

問 Where can I take a taxi?
我可以在哪裡招到計程車？

答 The taxi station is right on the corner.
計程車招呼站就在街角。

對方可以這麼說:

- ▶ Turn left and you will see the taxi station.
左轉你就會看到計程車招呼站。
- ▶ Turn right at the first corner.
在第一個轉彎處右轉。

▶ 搭計程車說明目的地

問 Where would you like to go?
您要去哪裡？

答 City Hall, please.
請到市政府。

你還可以這麼說:

- ▶ Can you get me out there?
你能不能載我去那邊？

► Please take me to this address.

請載我到這個地址。

► 車程有多遠

➪ How far is it from here?

從這裏過去有多遠？

➪ It is about 5 miles.

大約有五里。

► 搭計程車花費的時間

問 How long will it take?

需要多久的時間？

答 It's about 30 minutes.

大約卅分鐘。

你還可以這麼說:

► How long does it take to get there?

到哪裡要多久的時間？

▶ 儘速抵達

問 Can you get me to there in thirty minutes?
你可以在三十分鐘內送我到嗎？

答 Yes, sir.
是的，先生。

你還可以這麼說:

▶ Could you drive faster?
你能開快一點嗎？

▶ I have to be there by five o'clock.
我要在五點前到那裡。

▶ Can I get there by five o'clock?
我五點前到得了那裡嗎？

▶ 要下車

問 Let me off at the traffic light.
讓我在紅綠燈處下車。

答 Yes, sir.
好的，先生。

你還可以這麼說:

▶ Let me off at the third building.

讓我在第三棟大樓(前)下車。

▶ 抵達目的地

問 Here you are.

到了。

答 Is this the Seattle station?

這是西雅圖車站嗎？

▶ 計程車資

問 How much is the fare?

車資是多少？

答 Two hundred and fifty dollars.

二百五十元。

▶ 不用找零錢

問 It's two hundred dollars.

總共二百元。

答 Here you are. Keep the change.
錢在這裡。零錢不用找了。

▶ 公車總站在哪裡

問 Where is the bus station?
公車總站在哪裡？

答 Go straight ahead about four blocks, and you will see it.
直走四個街區，你就會看到。

▶ 搭公車的站數

問 How many stops are there to Seattle?
到西雅圖有多少個站？

答 That's the sixth stop.
那是第六個站。

你還可以這麼說:

▶ How many stops is it to Seattle?

從這裡到西雅圖要幾站？

▶ 搭哪一路公車

➪ Which bus could I get on to Seattle?
我應該搭哪一部公車去西雅圖？

➪ You can take the 265 or the 705.
你可以搭265號或705(公車)。

▶ 詢問公車路線

問 Does this bus go to City Hall?
這部公車有到市府嗎？

答 Yes, it goes to City Hall.
有的，有到市府。

你還可以這麼說:

▶ Does this bus go to the railway station?
這班公車有到火車站嗎？

▶ Is this the right bus to the railway station?
這是去火車站的公車嗎？

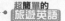

▶ 公車行經路線

問 Does the bus stop at the railway station?
這班公車有在火車站停嗎？

答 No. It only goes as far as the Western Hospital.
沒有。這班公車只到西區醫院。

你還可以這麼說:

- Is this bus stop for City Hall?
  這個站牌有(車)到市政府嗎？
- Does this bus stop at City Hall?
  這部公車有停在市政府嗎？

▶ 何處買公車票

問 Where can I buy the tickets?
哪裡可以買車票？

答 It's on the corner.
就在那個角落。

你還可以這麼說:

- Where can I buy a ticket to Seattle?
  哪裡可以買到西雅圖的車票？

▶ 發車的頻率

➪ How often does this bus run?
公車多久來一班？

➪ About ten minutes.
大約十分鐘。

▶ 什麼時候開車

問 When will the bus depart?
公車什麼時候開？

答 It starts out at 9 am.
九點就開車了。

你還可以這麼說:

▶ What time does the next bus for Seattle?
下一班到西雅圖的公車是什麼時候？

▶ 詢問車資

問 What is the fare?
車資是多少？

答 Fifty dollars per person.
一個人要五十元。

你還可以這麼說:

► What's the round-trip fare?
來回票是多少錢？

► 買公車票

問 I would like to buy a ticket to Seattle, please.
我要買一張到西雅圖的車票。

答 Fifty dollars.
五十元。

你還可以這麼說:

► A one-way/round-trip ticket to Seattle, please.
一張到西雅圖的單程/來回票。

► To Seattle for one adult and one child, please.
請給我一張大人一張小孩到西雅圖的票。

► Two tickets to Seattle, adult.
兩張到西雅圖的票，要成人票。

▶ 搭公車的車程

問 How long is the ride?
這一趟車程要多久?

答 It will take about twenty minutes.
大要需要二十分鐘。

你還可以這麼說:

► Is this a long ride?
車程要很長的時間嗎?

► How long does it take to get there?
到那裡要多久的時間?

► How long does this bus trip take?
坐公車要多久的時間?

▶ 在哪一站下車

問 Which stop should I get off at?
我應該哪一站下車?

答 You can get off at the Seattle Hospital.
你應該在西雅圖醫院下車。

你還可以這麼說:

▶ Where should I get off?

我要在哪裡下車？

▶ Where should I get off to go to Seattle?

到西雅圖我要在哪裡下車？

▶ 到站的時間預估

➪ When will I reach Seattle?
我什麼時候可以到西雅圖？

➪ About 5 pm.
大概下午五點鐘。

▶ 請求到站告知

問 Would you please tell me when we get there?
我們到達時可否告訴我一聲？

答 Of course.
當然好。

你還可以這麼說:

► Please tell me when to get off.

請告訴我何時要下車。

► 搭公車要求下車

問 Let me off here, please.

我要在這裡下車。

答 Sure.

好的。

► 如何搭火車

➪ Where should I get on the train?

我應該到哪裡搭火車？

➪ How do I get on the train?

我要如何搭火車？

► 搭哪一部列車

問 Which line should I take for Seattle?

我應該搭哪一線去西雅圖？

答 You can check the subway map over there.
你可以查在那裡的地鐵圖。

你還可以這麼說:

► Which train can I take to Seattle?
我要去西雅圖應該搭哪一列車？

► Which train goes to Seattle?
哪一班車廂到西雅圖？

► Is this the right line for New York?
去紐約是這條路線嗎？

► 在哪一個月台

問 Which platform is it on?
在哪一個月台？

答 The sixth platform.
第六月台

你還可以這麼說:

► Is this the right platform for New York?
這是出發到紐約的月台嗎？

▶ 在何處轉車

問 Where should I transfer to Seattle?

我要到哪裡轉車到西雅圖？

答 When you arrive at the Seattle Station, you get off and change the red line for Seattle.

當你到達西雅圖車站後下車，轉搭紅線到西雅圖。

你還可以這麼說:

▶ Where should I change the trains for New York?

去紐約要去哪裡換車？

▶ What train should I change to?

我要換哪一部車？

▶ 在車站內迷路

問 Which way should I go?

我應該走哪個方向？

答 Go down the stairs.

走樓梯下去。

對方可以這麼說:

▶ Just go down those steps.

只要走下樓梯就可以。

▶ Just take the escalator.

去搭手扶電梯。

▶ 在何處下車

⇨ Where should I get off at to go to New York?
到紐約要在哪裡下車？

▶ 租車訊息

問 I would like some information about renting a car.
我要知道一些租車的資訊。

答 What do you want to know?
您想要知道什麼？

▶ 租車費用

問 What's the rate for a car?
租一輛車要多少錢？

答 The daily rate is 1,500 dollars.
每天的租金是一千五百元。

對方可以這麼說:

▶ How much does it cost to rent a car?
租用一輛車需要多少錢？

▶ If I want to rent a van, how much would it cost?
如果我租一輛休旅車要多少錢？

▶ 租特定廠牌的車的費用

➪ What's the weekly rate for a Toyota?
租一輛豐田的車一星期要多少錢？

➪ It's 6,000 a week.
一個星期要六千元。

▶ 租車

問 I would like to rent a car.
我要租一輛車。

答 Do you have a reservation?
您有預約嗎？

你還可以這麼說:

► I'd like to rent a car one way.

我想租單程車

► 預約租車

問 Do you have a reservation?
您有預約嗎？

答 Yes, my name is David.
有，我的名字是大衛。

你還可以這麼說:

► I would like to reserve a Toyota for a week.

我要預約一個星期的豐田的車。

► 租車的種類

問 Which car would you like?
您要哪一種車？

答 I would like a Buick.
我要別克的車。

▶ 租車的時間

問 I will need it from this Monday to Friday.
我這個星期一到星期五需要這部車。

答 The daily rate is 1,500 dollars.
每天的租金是一千五百元。

你還可以這麼說:

▶ I would like to reserve this car for a week.
我要預約這輛車一個星期。

▶ 租車時填寫資料

問 I will need it from this Monday to Friday.
我這個星期一到星期五要租這部車。

答 OK. Now fill in this form and sign your name at the bottom.
好的，請填這份表格，然後在最下面簽上您的姓名。

▶ 租車時要求提供駕照

問 I want to rent a car.
我要租車。

答 Can I see your driver's license, please?
我能看你的駕照嗎？

▶ 還車的地點

問 Do I have to return the car here?
我要回到這裡還車嗎？

答 No. You may return it to our branches anywhere.
不必，你可以在我們任何地方的分公司還車。

▶ 租車費用的保證金

問 How much does it cost to rent a car?
租用一輛車需要多少錢？

答 You will have to use a credit card or leave a 500 deposit.
你需要用信用卡付費或先給五百元的保證金。

Unit 7 觀光

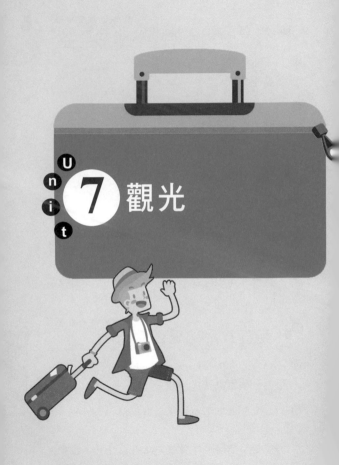

▶ 索取市區地圖

問 May I have a map of this city?
我可以要一張市區地圖嗎？

答 Yes. Here you are.
好的，給您。

你還可以這麼說:

▶ Do you have a map of the downtown?
你有市中心的地圖嗎？

▶ 索取旅遊手冊

問 Do you have any tour brochures?
你們有旅遊手冊嗎？

答 It's over there. Help yourself.
就在那裡，請自取。

你還可以這麼說:

▶ Where can I get some information on sightseeing tours?
那裡可以得到有關觀光旅遊的訊息？

▶ May I have some brochures for the city tours?

可以給我一些市區旅遊的簡介嗎？

▶ 索取訊息簡介

問 Which one has information about Cats?
哪一個有關於貓劇的訊息？

答 You probably need those brochures.
你可能需要這些簡介。

你還可以這麼說:

▶ Do you have a guide for plays?

你們有沒有戲劇指南？

▶ 詢問是否有當地旅遊團

問 Do you have any good package tours?
你們有好的套裝行程嗎？

答 Yes. We can arrange a city tour for you.
有的。我們可以幫您安排市區旅遊。

你還可以這麼說:

► Do you have any other tours that go to museums?

你們有任何去博物館的旅遊行程嗎？

► Is there any tour for Disneyland?

有沒有去迪士尼的旅遊行程？

► Can you arrange a night bus tour?

你可以安排夜間巴士旅遊嗎？

► 詢問行程安排

問 Are there any special places I should visit?
有沒有一些特殊的地方我應該去參觀？

答 How about the tour of the Central Park?
你覺得中央公園的行程如何？

你還可以這麼說:

► What tour should I take?

我應該參加哪一種行程？

► Is that building worth visiting?

那個大樓值得參觀嗎？

▶ 要求推薦旅遊行程

問 What tour do you recommend?

你推薦哪一種行程？

答 How about two-day tour? It includes Disneyland and sea cruise.

兩日遊行程如何？包括迪士尼樂園和海上旅遊。

你還可以這麼說：

- What sights do you recommend?

  你推薦哪一些觀光點？

- Which tour do you suggest?

  你建議哪一種旅遊團？

- Do you have any ideas about good sightseeing places?

  你知道任何不錯的觀光景點嗎？

▶ 推薦旅遊行程

問 It's only 500 dollars. You can visit the art gallery or the museum.
只要五百元。你可以參觀每一個美術館或博物館。

答 I would love to try.
我想試試看。

你還可以這麼說:

▶ I am interested in this tour.
我對這個行程有興趣。

▶ 詢問旅遊行程的內容

問 Does this tour include the art gallery?
旅遊行程有包括美術館嗎？

答 No, it just passes by the art gallery.
沒有，只有經過美術館而已。

你還可以這麼說:

▶ Will we visit the City Hall?

我們會參觀市府嗎？

▶ What dose it include in that night tour?

夜間旅遊包含哪些？

▶ Does this tour include the Grand Canyon?

這個旅遊行程有包含大峽谷嗎？

▶ Does this tour go to the National Park?

這個旅遊行程有去國家公園嗎？

▶ 旅遊行程的種類

問 What kind of tour do you have?

你們有哪一種行程？

答 There are 3 tours, Disneyland, Museum, and Casino.

有三種旅遊團，迪士尼樂園、博物館和賭場。

你還可以這麼說:

▶ How do you like sightseeing buses?

你覺得市區巴士觀光如何？

▶ How about the Statue of Liberty?

你覺得自由女神像如何？

▶ 旅遊行程花費的時間

問 How many days does this city tour take?
這個市區行程要多久的時間？

答 It'll take 2 days.
要兩天的時間。

對方可以這麼說:

▶ How many hours does it take?

要花幾個小時的時間？

▶ What time will it be over?

幾點會結束？

▶ How long will it be?

會是多久的時間？

▶ 旅遊團的預算

問 What's your budget?
你們的預算是多少？

答 Not too much. It's about 4 thousand.
不太多。大約四千元。

你還可以這麼說:

▶ We have to keep budget below 1,000 dollars.
我們需要把預算控制在一千元以下。

▶ 旅遊團費用

問 What's the price of the half day tour?
半天的旅遊行程要多少錢？

答 It's 2,000 dollars for one person.
每一個人兩千元。

你還可以這麼說:

▶ What's the price for that tour?
那個旅遊行程多少錢？

▶ What's the price of the full-day city tour?
一日遊的行程費用是多少？

▶ 人數、身分不同的團費

問 How much will it cost for kids?

小孩子要多少錢？

答 It's 1,000 dollars for one kid.

小孩子每一個人一千元。

你還可以這麼說:

▶ What's the price for an adult?

大人的費用要多少？

▶ How much will it cost for one person?

一個人要多少錢？

▶ 旅遊團費用明細

問 Is the tour all-inclusive?

行程包括所有的費用嗎？

答 Yes, the round-trip fare, and the meals are included.

是的，包括來回車資和餐費。

對方可以這麼說:

▶ Is there any meals included?

有包含餐點嗎？

► Does this price include meals?

這個價錢有包含餐點嗎？

► Does it include an English speaking guide?

有包括會說英文的導遊嗎？

► 旅遊接送服務

問 Is there a pick up service at the hotel?

有沒有到飯店接送呢？

答 Yes, the guide will pick you up in the lobby.

是的，導遊會在大廳等你。

► 詢問集合的時間與地點

問 Where and when shall we meet?

我們何地何時集合？

答 In front of the station, 9 am.

車站前，九點鐘

► 旅遊團出發的時間

問 What time does the tour start?

旅遊團幾點開始？

答 The bus meets in front of the hotel at 9 am.
巴士早上九點在飯店前集合。

對方可以這麼說:

► The tour guide will be here to pick you up around 9 o'clock.
導遊會在九點鐘左右來這裡接你。

► 預約旅遊團

問 Can I make a reservation here for tomorrow?
我能在這裡預約明天（行程）嗎？

答 Sure. May I have your name, please?
好的。請給我您的大名。

你還可以這麼說:

► Could you reserve this tour for two of us?
你能幫我們預約兩個人的這個旅遊行程嗎？

▶ 參加當地旅遊團

問 I am interested in the art gallery tour.

我對博物館行程有興趣。

答 OK. Here is the registration form. Please fill it in.

好的，這是登記表格，請先填寫。

你還可以這麼說:

▶ I would like to join the full-day city tour.

我要參加市內的一日遊行程。

▶ I would like to join the city tour.

我想要參加市內旅行團。

▶ I would like to join the Casino.

我要參加賭場的行程。

▶ I would like to join the sea cruise tomorrow.

我要參加明天的旅艇行程。

▶ I would like to join this city night tour.

我要參加市區夜間旅遊。

▶ I would rather go on a half-day tour.

我比較想參加半天的行程。

▶ 旅遊團自由活動的時間

問 We'll have a thirty-minute break now.
我們現在有卅分鐘的休息時間。

答 How long are we staying here?
我們要在這裡停留多久？

你還可以這麼說:

► Do we have time to drop in at the art gallery?
我們有空進去美術館看看嗎？

► Do we have time to buy some souvenirs?
我們有時間買一些紀念品嗎？

▶ 自由活動結束的時間

問 When shall we come back here?
我們要幾點回來？

答 Please come back on the bus by 11 o'clock.
請在十一點前回到巴士上。

▶ 門票

問 What's the admission fee?
門票是多少？

答 It' s 500 dollars per person.
一個人要五百元。

你還可以這麼說:

▶ Is the admission fee included?
門票都是有包括（在費用內）嗎？

▶ 詢問上演的節目

➪ What opera is performing tonight?
今晚上演哪一部歌劇？

➪ It's Cats.
是貓劇。

▶ 詢問開始及結束的時間

問 What time does this show start?
這場秀什麼時候開始？

答 At 7 o'clock.

在七點鐘（開始）。

你還可以這麼說:

▶ What time does this show end?

這場秀什麼時候結束？

▶ 詢問是否可以拍照

問 Can we take pictures in the museum?

我們可以在美術館裡拍照嗎？

答 Go ahead.

請便。

你還可以這麼說:

▶ Can I take a picture here?

我可以在這裡拍照嗎？

▶ Can I take a picture for you?

我可以幫你拍一張照片嗎？

▶ 詢問是否可以幫忙拍照

問 Would you please take a picture for me?
可以請您幫我拍一張照片嗎？

答 Sure.
好啊。

你還可以這麼說:

▶ Would you mind taking my picture?
您介意幫我拍一張照片嗎？

▶ 參加當地旅遊的常見問題

➪ What does that mean?
那是什麼意思？

➪ How do you call it in English?
英文怎麼說那個東西？

➪ Would you please explain it to me?
你能解釋給我聽嗎？

English For Travel

Unit 8 尋求協助

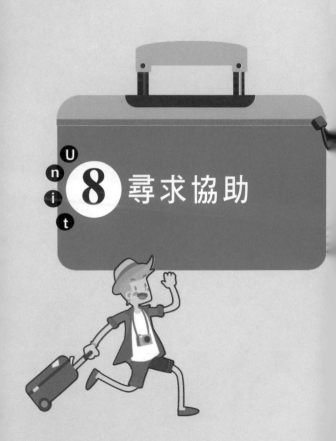

▶ 尋求協助

問 Please do me a favor.

請幫我一個忙。

答 What's it?

要幫什麼忙？

你還可以這麼說:

▶ Give me a hand, please.

請幫我一個忙。

▶ Would you please help me?

能請你幫我一個忙嗎？

▶ I need your help.

我需要你的幫忙。

▶ 救命時

➪ Help!

救命啊！

➪ Please call the police.

請叫警察。

➪ Please call 911.

請報警。(美國地區適用)

▶ 請對方再說一次

問 Please move over.

請移過去一點。

答 Pardon?

請再說一次。

你還可以這麼說:

► Excuse me?

你說什麼？

► What did you just say?

你剛剛說什麼？

▶ 提出要求時

問 What can I do for you?

需要我協助嗎？

答 May I use your telephone?

我能借用你的電話嗎？

你還可以這麼說:

▶ May I …?

我可以…？

▶ Could I …?

我能夠…？

▶ 提出問題時

問 What can I do for you?

需要我協助嗎？

答 Do you know what it is?

你知道這是什麼嗎？

你還可以這麼說:

▶ Do you know how to say it in English?

你知道英文要怎麼說嗎？

▶ 問路

問 Excuse me. Where is the Custom Tour Center?

請問，旅客旅遊中心在哪裡？

答 It's right on the corner of the first street.
就在第一街的角落。

你還可以這麼說:

- Where is the museum?
  博物館在哪裡？
- Where is the duty-free shop?
  免稅店在哪裡？
- Where is the restroom?
  洗手間在哪裡？

▶ 問方向

問 Would you show me how to get there?
你可以告訴我如何去那裡嗎？

答 Turn right and you will see it.
右轉你就會看到。

你還可以這麼說:

- How do I get to Taipei?
  我要怎麼去台北？

▶ How do I get to the City Hall?

我要怎麼去市府？

▶ Could you give me directions to the City Hall?

你可以告訴我去市府的方向嗎？

▶ What direction should I follow to get to the City Hall?

哪一個方向可以去市府？

▶ 問地點

問 Is there a police station near here?
這附近有警察局嗎？

答 Yes, there is. Go straight and you will see it on your right.
有，在那兒。一直往前走你就會看到在你的右手邊。

你還可以這麼說:

▶ Where's the restroom?

洗手間在哪兒？

▶ Where's the nearest police station?

離這兒最近的警察局在哪裡？

▶ Is there a police station around here?

這附近有警察局嗎？

▶ Do you know of any police stations near here?

您知道這附近有任何警察局嗎？

▶ 說明路程

問 Where is the police station?

警察局在哪兒?

答 Go straight for two blocks.

一直走，過兩條街就有。

對方可以這麼說:

▶ Turn right and go straight ahead.

左轉再直走。

▶ Go through the door.

穿過門就到了。

▶ It's on your left hand.

在你的左手邊

▶ Make a right at the light.

在紅綠燈右轉。

▶ Turn right at the first traffic light.

在第一個紅綠燈右轉。

▶ Go straight ahead until the traffic light and it's on your right hand.

直走到紅綠燈，就在你的右手邊。

▶ 走錯路

問 Is this the way to the station?

這是去車站的路嗎？

答 You are going the wrong way.

你走錯路了。

▶ 迷路

問 May I help you?

需要我幫忙嗎？

答 I'm lost.

我迷路了。

你還可以這麼說:

▶ I don't know where I am.

我不知道我現在身在何處？

► What street am I on?

我現在在哪條街上？

► Where am I on this map?

我在地圖上的什麼地方？

► Where am I?

我在哪兒呢？

► Where am I located?

我在什麼地方呢？

► 指出所在地

問 Excuse me. I am lost.

抱歉，我迷路了。

答 You're right here, near the station.

你在這兒，在車站附近。

► 指出相關地點所在地

問 Yes, I am lost. Do you know where the Museum is?

是的，我迷路了。你知道博物館在哪裡嗎？

答 It's next to the coffee shop.

在那家咖啡館的旁邊。

你還可以這麼說:

- It's across from the City Hall.
  在市府的對面。
- It's on the opposite side of the City Hall.
  正對著市府。
- It's between the bookstore and the station.
  在書店和車站之間。
- It's on this side of the church.
  在教堂的這一邊。
- It's at the end of this street.
  在這條路的盡頭。

▶ 明顯地標

問 What are the landmarks around the station?
車站附近有沒有明顯的建築物?

答 There is a red building next to the station.
車站旁有一棟紅色的建築物。

▶ 車子拋錨

➪ Could you help jump-start my car?
可以用你車上的電瓶幫我發動車子嗎？

➪ I have a flat tire.
我的輪胎沒氣了。

➪ My car broke down on the freeway.
我的車在高速公路上拋錨了。

➪ There is something wrong with my car.
我的車出了一點問題。

➪ My car won't start.
我的車就是發不動。

➪ We have a flat tire here.
我們的車爆胎了。

➪ My car broke down.
我的車壞了！

▶ 車子發生擦撞

問 What seems to be the problem with your car?
你的車是哪裡有問題啊？

答 Let's not argue.
我們不要吵了。

▶ 車子加油

➪ Fill'er up!
加滿！

Unit 9 和警察的互動

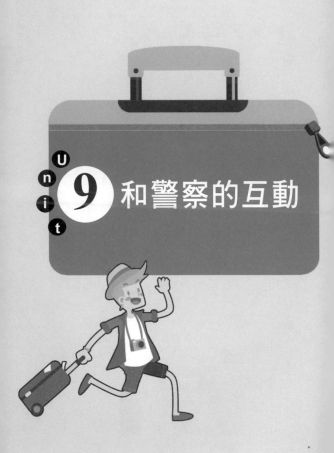

▶ 被警察詢問是否有證件

問 Do you bring your ID card with you?
你身上有帶你的身分證嗎？

答 Yes, I do.
有的，我有帶。

對方可以這麼說:

► Do you bring any identifications?
你有帶任何的證件嗎？

► Where is your ID card?
你的身分證呢？

▶ 被警察要求要求看證件

問 Identification, please.
證件給我。

答 Sorry, officer, I forgot to bring my ID card with me.
警官，抱歉，我忘記帶身分證。

對方可以這麼說:

► Show me your ID.

證件給我看。

► Can I see your identification, please?

我可以看一下你的證件嗎？

► 被警察要求要求看護照

問 What's wrong?

怎麼啦？

答 Let me see your passport.

讓我看看你的護照。

對方可以這麼說:

► Let me see your passport and visa.

讓我看看你的護照和簽證。

► What is your passport number?

你的護照號碼是幾號？

▶ 提供證件給警察

問 Can I see your identification, please?
我可以看一下你的證件嗎？

答 Yes. Here you are.
好的，在這裡。

你還可以這麼說:

► I don't have any ID with me.
我沒有帶任何的證件。

► Can I show you my international driver's license?
我可以給你看我的國際駕照嗎？

▶ 被警察質疑證件

問 This is not your ID card.
這不是你的身分證。

答 It's mine.
這是我的。

對方可以這麼說:

▶ You are showing me the false identification, aren't you?

你給我假的證件，對吧？

▶ Are you sure this is your ID card?

你確定這是你的身分證？

▶ 證件過期

問 Your passport expired.

你的護照過期了。

答 Really? That must be a mistake.

真的？一定是弄錯了吧！

對方可以這麼說:

▶ Your license will expire tomorrow.

你的駕照明天就要過期了。

▶ This certificate is valid for three months.

這個證件有效期是三個月。

▶ Your deriver's license has expired, so it is invalid.

你的駕照過期了，所以這是無效的。

▶ 被警察告知違法

問 We believe you have broken the law.
我們深信你已經違法了。

答 I did nothing wrong.
我沒做錯事。

對方可以這麼說:

▶ I am afraid you already broke the law.
恐怕你已經違法了。

▶ It's illegal.
這是違規。

▶ 被警察說明禁止事件

問 I can't do it here?
我不能在這裡做這件事？

答 No, you can't. It is forbidden to fish here.
不可以。這塊海域內禁止垂釣。

對方可以這麼說:

▶ No, you can't. It is forbidden to spit on the ground.
不可以。這裡禁止隨地吐痰。

► No, you can't. Swimming is not allowed at this beach.

不可以。這片海灘禁止游泳。

► No, you can't. This is non-smoking area.

不可以。這裡抽是禁菸區。

► 違法事件

問 What's going on here?

這裡發生什麼事了？

答 It is against the law.

這是違法的。

對方可以這麼說:

► It's still against the law.

那還是違法的。

► Do you realize it is against the law?

你知道這是違法的嗎？

► 涉及案件

問 What did I do?

我做了什麼？

答 You are suspected of homicide.
你涉有殺人罪嫌。

對方可以這麼說:

► We believe you have committed a crime.
我們相信你有犯罪。

► You will be charged with possessing illegal drugs.
你將以持有毒品被起訴。

► 違反法律

問 Did I break the law?
我有犯法嗎？

答 It is forbidden to do so in the USA.
在美國禁止這樣的行為。

對方可以這麼說:

► According to the law, it's forbidden.
根據法律，這是禁止的。

▶ 違法的罰單

問 I have to give you a ticket.
我必須開你一張罰單。

答 I am sorry, but I didn't do it on purpose.
抱歉，我不是故意這麼做的。

對方可以這麼說:

▶ I'm afraid I'm going to give you a ticket.
恐怕我得要開你一張罰單。

▶ I'm going to write you a ticket.
我要開罰單給你。

▶ This is your ticket.
這是你的罰單。

▶ 違法的罰款

問 If you smoke in the MRT, you have to pay a fine.
如果你在捷運站內抽煙，你要被罰款。

答 I am really sorry. I won't do it again.
我真的很抱歉，我不會再這麼做了。

對方可以這麼說:

- Riding without wearing a helmet is a five hundred dollars fine.
  騎機車未戴安全帽，罰五佰元。
- You are fined three hundred dollars.
  你被罰款三百元。
- You will be fined if you spit on the streets.
  你如果在街上吐痰，會遭罰款的。

▶ 警察表明身分

問 Who are you?

你們是誰？

答 Police!

（我們是）警察！

對方可以這麼說:

- Freeze! Police!
  不准動！我是警察！

▶ 警察要求動作

問 Hands up!

手舉起來！

答 I will do what you said.

我會照著你說的做。

對方可以這麼說:

► On your knees!

跪下！

► Get down!

蹲下！

► Get down on the ground!

趴在地上！

► Get back!

退後！

► Come here!

過來！

► Get into the car.

上車。

► Turn around slowly!

慢慢地轉身！

► 警察要求看見雙手

問 Let me see your hands.

讓我看到你的雙手。

答 I will do what you said.
我會照著你說的做。

對方可以這麼說:

- Put your hands where I can see.
  把你的手放在我可以看得見的地方。
- Put your hands on your head.
  把雙手放在頭上。
- Take your hands out of your pockets slowly.
  慢慢地把你的手從口袋裡拿出來。

▶ 被警察喝阻放下武器

問 Drop your weapon!
放下武器！

答 I am going to drop it down.
我要放下了。

你還可以這麼說:

- I will do what you said.
  我會照做。

► No problem.

沒問題。

► OK, OK.

好，好。

► 被警察喝阻不准動

問 Freeze!

不准動！

答 Don't shoot.

不要開槍。

對方可以這麼說:

► Halt or I'll shoot!

不要動，不然我要開槍！

► Don't move!

不准動！

► Stay where you are.

站在原地。

▶ 被逮捕

問 You are under arrest!

你被捕了！

答 I want to see my lawyer.

我要見我的律師。

你還可以這麼說:

► What did I do? It must be a mistake.

我做了什麼事？你們一定弄錯了。

► What happened?

發生了什麼事？

► What's going on?

怎麼了？

► Hey, what's the matter?

嘿，怎麼回事？

▶ 被銬上手銬

問 I am going to put handcuffs on you.

我要把你銬上手銬。

答 You can't do this to me.

你不能這麼對我。

你還可以這麼說:

▶ Easy. It hurts.

輕一點，很痛的。

▶ 被拘留

問 You have no right to arrest me.

你們沒有權力逮捕我。

答 We have an arrest warrant.

我們有拘票！

對方可以這麼說:

▶ We can keep you in lock-up for about twenty-four hours.

我們可以把你拘留廿四小時。

▶ 被搜索住處

問 Where is your warrant?

你們的搜索令呢？

答 This is a warrant issued by a court.

這是法院發出的搜查令。

對方可以這麼說：

► We are police officers. Let us in.
我們是警察，讓我們進去。

► We have a search warrant.
我們有搜索票！

► We have a warrant to search your house.
我們有搜索令可以搜查你的房子。

► 警察宣讀權利

問 I didn't kill him.
我沒有殺他。

答 Do you understand your rights?
你是否了解你的權利？

對方可以這麼說：

► You have the right to remain silent.
你有權保持緘默。

► Anything you tell the police may be used against you later in court.
你對警察所言會當成呈堂證供。

► You don't have to say anything.
你不必說任何事情。

▶ 被帶至警察局

問 We are going to take you to the police station.

我們要帶你去警察局。

答 I am innocent.

我是無辜的。

你還可以這麼說:

▶ You can't do this to me.

你們不能這樣對待我。

▶ 要求有律師在場

問 We can't release you without permission.

沒有允許，我們不能釋放你。

答 I need a lawyer.

我需要一位律師。

你還可以這麼說:

▶ I want to see my lawyer.

我要見我的律師。

► I want to see my lawyer now.

我現在就要見我的律師。

► 提出其他要求

問 You are accused of murder.

你被指控犯了殺人罪。

答 I want to make a phone call.

我要打電話。

你 還可以這麼說:

► I want to see our ambassador.

我要見我們的大使。

► I want to see my parents.

我要見我的父母。

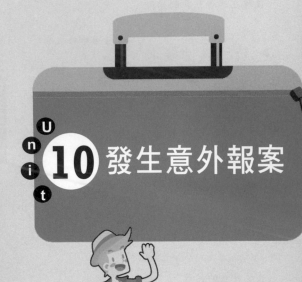

Unit 10 發生意外報案

▶ 備案

問 Do you want to file a report?
你要備案嗎？

答 Yes, my friend just had a car accident.
是的，我的朋友剛發生車禍。

你還可以這麼說:

- Yes, there's a robbery at the Maple Avenue.
  在楓葉大道發生一起搶案。
- Yes, someone had a heart attack on the corner of Maple and Lucky.
  有一個人在楓葉路和幸運路的轉角處心臟病發作。
- Yes, I witnessed the traffic accident.
  我目睹了交通事故。

▶ 報案

問 What do you want to report?
你要報什麼案件？

答 My father burned his hand.
我的父親燒傷他的手。

你還可以這麼說:

- My friend had a car accident at the Maple Road and the First Avenue.
我的朋友在楓葉路和第一大道發生車禍。
- There is a fire in my building at the First Street.
在第一街我住的大樓發生火災。

▶ 至警察局報案

問 I want to report a robbery.
我要報一件搶案。

答 Please fill out this form.
請填寫這份表格。

▶ 說明自己的遭遇

問 What happened to you?
你發生什麼事了？

答 Two men just robbed me.
剛才我被兩個人搶劫。

你 還可以這麼說:

► Someone stole my wallet a few minutes ago.
我的皮包幾分鐘前被扒走了。

► Someone attacked me.
有人攻擊我。

► I was assaulted.
我被攻擊了。

► 案件發生的始末

問 How did it happen?
這件事怎麼發生的？

答 I have no idea. It happened so suddenly.
我也不知知道。事情發生得太突然了。

你 還可以這麼說:

► He beat me for no reason.
他毫無理由就打我。

► There was a man tried to rape me.

有一個男人企圖強暴我。

► They suddenly assaulted me.

他們突然攻擊我。

► They said nothing, and took away my bags.

他們沒有說什麼，就拿走我的背包。

► 電話報案

問 There is a murder in my building.

我的大樓發生謀殺案。

答 Stay where you are.

你待在原處。

對方可以這麼說:

► We will send an officer there.

我們會派警察過去。

► We will be there soon.

我們(警察)很快就會過去。

▶ 說明刑事案件內容

問 What happened to you?
你怎麼啦？

答 I was robbed at the First Avenuc yesterday.
我昨天在第一大道被搶劫。

你還可以這麼說:

▶ My child was kidnapped.
我的孩子被綁架了。

▶ He snatched away my bag.
他搶走我的袋子。

▶ Someone broke into my house.
有人闖進我家。

▶ Someone pointed a gun at me.
有一個人拿槍對著我。

▶ 物品遺失

問 What do you want to report?
你要報什麼案件？

答 I have lost my bag.
我把袋子弄丟了。

你還可以這麼說:

► I left my bag in a cab.

我把袋子遺失在計程車上。

► I lost my wallet somewhere in the park this morning.

我今天早上在公園的某個地方掉了皮夾。

► 孩子失蹤

問 My kid was missing.
我的孩子失蹤了。

答 Do you have any pictures of your kid?
你有任何孩子的照片嗎？

你還可以這麼說:

► I can't find my kids.

我找不到我的孩子們。

▶ 目擊案件發生

問 Did you witness the accident?
你有目擊意外發生嗎？

答 Yes, I was standing right therc.
有的，我就站在那裡。

你還可以這麼說:

▶ Yes, I was talking to that victim at that moment.
有的，我當時和被害人在說話。

▶ 描述犯人面貌、衣著

問 What did the suspect look like?
嫌犯長什麼樣子？

答 His face is thin and tanned.
他的面孔削瘦，曬得很黑。

你還可以這麼說:

▶ He has long brown hair.
他有一頭褐色長髮。

▶ He has brown eyes.

他的眼睛是棕色的。

▶ It's a guy in black.

是個穿黑衣的男人。

▶ He is about thirties in red shirt.

他大約三十多歲，身穿紅襯衫。

▶ 描述犯人體型

問 Can you give me a description?

可以形容一下他的樣子嗎？

答 He was about six feet tall.

他大概六呎高。

你還可以這麼說:

▶ He is a tall and fat guy.

他是個又高又胖的男人。

▶ The thief is a tall man in his mid forties.

小偷身材高大，大約四十五歲左右。

▶ 猜測犯人的年紀

問 What do you say how old he is?
你想他的年紀是多少？

答 He is about forties.
他大約四十多歲。

你還可以這麼說:

- ► He looks in his mid twenties.
  他看起來廿五歲左右。
- ► He is so young.
  他很年輕。
- ► He is a teenager.
  他是個十幾歲的青少年。

▶ 猜測犯人的身分

問 Is the suspect a white?
嫌疑犯是白人嗎？

答 He is a black.
他是一位黑人。

你還可以這麼說:

► He is a white male.

他是一位白人男性。

► He is an Asian with beard.

他是一個蓄著山羊鬍的亞洲人。

► 沒有目擊案件發生

問 Did you see that guy?
你看到了那個人嗎？

答 I saw nothing.
我什麼都沒有看到。

你還可以這麼說:

► No. It's dark.

沒有，天很黑。

► 目擊證人的指認

問 Can you identify him?
你能指認他嗎？

答 Yes, I recognize him.

可以，我認得他。

對方可以這麼說:

► Can you identify the suspect?

你可以指認那個嫌犯嗎？

► Would you mind being a witness?

你願意當證人嗎？

► 說明案件發生過程

問 Can you describe it in detail?

能請你詳細描述當時情形嗎？

答 That big guy kept trying to talk to me. Then I found my wallet was gone.

那個大個子男人一直試圖跟我說話。然後我發現我的皮夾不見了。

對方可以這麼說:

► How did the suspect assault you?

嫌犯怎麼攻擊你？

► Why did he attack you?

他為什麼要攻擊你？

▶ Did you attempt to defend yourself?

你曾企圖自衛嗎？

▶ Did you attempt to run away?

你曾企圖逃跑嗎？

▶ Did any strangers try to talk to you?

有沒有任何陌生人試著跟你說話？

▶ 案件發生地點

問 Where did this incident occur?

這件事是在什麼地方發生的？

答 In front of the train station.

在車站前面。

你還可以這麼說:

▶ Inside the MRT.

在捷運站裡面。

▶ At the bank.

在銀行。

▶ At a restaurant.

在一家餐廳。

▶ 案件發生時間

問 What time did this accident occur?
這件事故是什麼時候發生的？

答 After I stepped out of the building.
在我步出大樓後。

你還可以這麼說:

- It's about 8 am.
大約早上八點。
- At night.
在晚上（發生）。
- When I made dinner.
當我煮晚餐的時候。

▶ 警方安撫

問 I am so scared.
我好害怕。

答 We will take care of everything.
我們會處理一切的。

對方可以這麼說:

► We will do our best.

我們會盡力。

► We will help you.

我們會幫你的。

► Calm down.

冷靜下來。

► 要求警察抓回歹徒

問 Will you seize that robber?
你們會抓回搶劫者嗎？

答 We will patrol this area more often than before.
我們會比以前更加強這一帶的巡邏。

English For Travel

Unit 11 交通事故

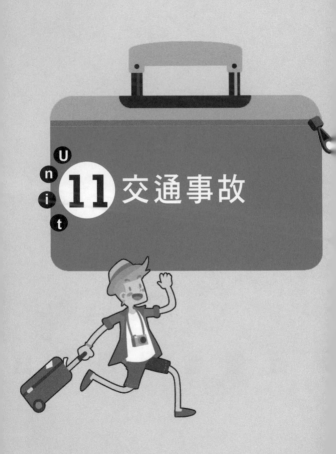

▶ 被攔檢

問 Pull over.

停車！

答 What's wrong?

有什麼不對嗎？

你還可以這麼說:

▶ What happened?

發生什麼事了？

▶ What did I do?

我做了什麼？

▶ Did I do something against the law?

我違規了嗎？

▶ Am I in trouble?

我有什麼麻煩了嗎？

▶ 面對交通臨檢

問 Something wrong?

發生什麼事了？

答 This is a traffic check.

這是交通臨檢。

對方可以這麼說:

▶ This is a routine examination.

這是例行的檢查。

▶ This is a routine job.

這是例行的工作。

▶ 警察說明臨檢的原因

問 Did I do something wrong?
我有做錯事嗎？

答 We are doing a vehicle check.
我們正在做汽機車臨檢。

對方可以這麼說:

▶ We are having a traffic security check.

我們正在做交通安全臨檢。

▶ We are looking for a criminal.

我們正在搜尋罪犯。

▶ We are looking for an escapee from the prison.

我們正在搜尋一名逃獄犯。

▶ 被要求配合臨檢

問 Step outside, please.
請出來。

答 Yes, sir.
好的，警官。

對方可以這麼說:

▶ Keep your hands on the steering wheel.
把手放在方向盤上。

▶ Just remain inside your car.
請留在車內。

▶ Were you drinking tonight?
你今晚有喝酒嗎？

▶ Please roll down your window.
請搖下車窗。

▶ 被臨檢時要求搜查車子

問 What's wrong, officer?
警官，發生什麼事了？

答 We need to search your car.
我們要搜查您的車子。

對方可以這麼說:

► Open your trunk, please.
請打開行李廂。

► Please show me your storage compartment.
請讓我看你的置物箱。

► 告訴警察自己要拿證件

問 May I look for my ID?
我可以找找我的證件嗎?

答 Please do it.
請便。

► 詢問警官身分

問 May I know your name, badge number and jurisdiction?
我能知道你的姓名、警徽號碼及管轄範圍嗎?

答 Here is my police ID.
這是我的警察證件。

▶ 被警察要求看駕照

問 Your driver's license, please.
給我你的駕照。

答 Here you are.
在這裡

對方可以這麼說:

- And your vehicle registration, please.
  還有你的汽車行照（給我）。
- Please show me your driver's license and vehicle registration.
  請出示你的駕照及行照。
- I need to see your driver's license.
  我必須看一下你的駕照。

▶ 警察說明看證件的原因

問 Why do you want to see my ID card?
你為什麼要看我的身分證？

答 This is a routine job.
這是例行的工作。

對方可以這麼說:

► We are looking for someone.

我們正在搜尋一個人。

► 詢問看駕照的原因

問 I need to see your driver's license.

我必須看一下你的駕照。

答 What for?

要做什麼用？

你還可以這麼說:

► Why?

為什麼？

► How come?

為什麼？

► 詢問警察的回應

問 What are you checking with your computer?

你在用電腦查什麼？

答 To check and see if you are a reported missing person or a wanted criminal.
看看你是不是通報失蹤人口或懸賞的罪犯。

▶ 證件過期

➪ Your license will expire tomorrow.
你的駕照明天要過期了。

➪ Your driver's license already expired.
你的駕照已經過期了。

➪ Your license expired on the last day of September.
你的駕照在九月卅日過期了。

➪ Your vehicle registration will expire on September.
你的行照今年九月就要到期了喔！

➪ Your vehicle insurance expired last month.
你的車險上個月過期了。

▶ 不知自己證件過期

問 Your driver's license already expired on September.
你的駕照已經在九月過期了。

答 Really? Let me see.
真的？我瞧瞧。

你還可以這麼說:

▶ I don't think so.
不會吧？
▶ Thank you for reminder.
謝謝你的提醒。
▶ Please don't write me a ticket.
請不要開我罰單。

▶ 為證件過期找藉口

問 Your license expired last week.
你的駕照在上星期就過期了。

答 But it's only a few days out of date, officer.
警官，只有過期幾天啊！

你還可以這麼說:

▶ I really don't know about it, officer.
警官，我真的不知道這件事。

▶ 被質疑不是車主

問 Do you own this car?
你是車主嗎？

答 Of course, officer. It's my car.
當然是啊，警官。 這是我的車子。

對方可以這麼說:

▶ Is this your car, sir?

先生，這是你的車子嗎？

▶ May I see the owner's ID for the vehicle?

我可以看這輛車的車主身分證件嗎？

▶ 車籍資料

問 Here is my vehicle registration.
這是我的行照。

答 This is not the vehicle registration of this motorbike.
這不是這部機車的行照。

對方可以這麼說:

▶ This vehicle registration number doesn't belong to this car.

這個行照號碼不是這輛車的。

▶ 被質疑為贓車

問 Yes, sir?

警官，有什麼事？

答 Where did you get this car?

你這輛車哪裡來的？

對方可以這麼說:

▶ This is a stolen car.

這是一輛失竊的車。

▶ 車子所有權

問 Is the fifty-one eighty-one DG your car?

（車號）5181DG是你的車嗎？

答 Yes, it's my car.

對，是我的車子。

你還可以這麼說:

▶ No. I rend it.

不是。我租的。

▶ No, it's not my vehicle.

不是，這不是我的車。

▶ No, mine is over there, fifty-eight fifty-one CH.

不是，我的車子是在那裡，（車號）5851CH。

▶ 不知已違反交通規則

問 Is it illegal?

這是違規的嗎？

答 Yes, you already broke the traffic laws.

是的，你已經違反交通規則了。

你還可以這麼說:

▶ I can't turn right here?

我不能在這裡右轉？

▶ 被要求停車

問 Stop!

停車！

答 What's up, sir?

警官，有什麼事？

對方可以這麼說:

▶ Pull over.

靠邊停車！

▶ Turn off the car.

把車子熄火！

▶ 警察說明違規事項

問 You were driving in a bus lane.

你駕駛在公車道上。

答 I don't know this is a bus lane.

我不知道這是公車道。

對方可以這麼說:

- You made an illegal left turn.
  你違規左轉。
- You just ran a red light.
  你剛闖紅燈。
- You made an illegal U-turn.
  你違規迴轉。
- Do you realize it's parked in a no parking zone?
  你可知道你停在禁止停車的地方？
- You may not use cellular phones while driving.
  開車不得使用行動電話。

▶ 堅稱沒有違規

問 Please step out of the car.
請下車。

答 I didn't break the law.
我沒有違規。

你還可以這麼說:

► I did nothing wrong.

我沒有做錯事。

► 為違規找理由

問 It's illegally parked. Do you see the red line?

這是違規停車。你有看到紅線吧？

答 Yes, but I just parked for two minutes.

是啊，可是我只停兩分鐘而已。

你還可以這麼說:

► But they told me I could park here.

但是他們告訴我可以停在這裡。

► 配合警察要求

問 Please roll down your window.

請把車窗搖下。

答 Did I break the traffic law?

我有違規嗎？

對方可以這麼說:

► Please step out of your car.

請下車。

► 被要求駛離現場

問 You can't stop here!

你不能在這裡停車。

答 Sorry, officer.

抱歉，警官。

對方可以這麼說:

► Please remove your car from here.

請把你的車駛離現場。

► 警察要求作酒測

問 I need to do a few tests.

我要做一些測試。

答 I am not drunk.

我沒有喝醉。

對方可以這麼說:

► I am going to ask you some questions.

我要問你一些問題。

► I want you to do some tests.

我要你做一些測試。

► 違規後的處理

問 What should I do now?
我現在應該要做什麼?

答 You are free to go.
你可以走了。

對方可以這麼說:

► You can go now.

你可以離開了。

► You are not free to leave.

你不可以離開。

► 禁止停車

問 It is no parking here.
這裡禁止停車。

答 OK. I remove it now.
好的，我現在就開走。

對方可以這麼說:

▶ This is a no parking zone.
這裡是禁止停車區。

▶ Your car is double-parked.
你併排停車。

▶ Don't stop your car on the tracks.
不要將你的車子停在鐵軌上。

▶ 違規停車

問 You couldn't park by a fire hydrant.
你不能停在消防栓旁。

答 Sorry. I will drive away right now.
抱歉，我馬上開走。

你還可以這麼說:

▶ I am so sorry. I didn't notice that.
很抱歉，我沒注意到。

▶ 違規規勸

問 It's dangerous and against the law.
這很危險，而且違法。

答 Thank you, officer. I won't do it again.
謝謝你，警官。我不會再犯了。

對方可以這麼說:

- ► You are driving too slowly.
你開太慢了。
- ► You have too many people in your car.
你超載了。
- ► You were not wearing your seat-belt.
你沒繫安全帶。
- ► You cannot drive without a license.
你不可以無照駕駛。

▶ 闖越路口

問 Why do you stop my car?
你為什麼攔下我的車？

答 You just jaywalked across the street.
你剛剛違規穿越馬路。

對方可以這麼說:

► You went through a level crossing.

你闖越平交道。

► You went through an intersection.

你闖越路口。

► 違規肇事

問 What did I do, officer?
警官，我做了什麼事？

答 You went through a stop sign and hit a car.
你闖紅燈又撞了一輛車。

對方可以這麼說:

► You hit a pedestrian.

你撞到一個路人了。

► 機車違規

問 You are riding without a helmet.
你騎機車未戴安全帽。

答 But my helmet was just stolen.
可是我的安全帽被偷了。

你還可以這麼說:

► Sorry, I forgot to wear it.
抱歉，我忘了戴。

► 違規右轉

問 Was I speeding?
我超速了嗎？

答 No, but you made an illegal right turn.
沒有，但是你違規右轉了。

你還可以這麼說:

► I thought I could turn there.
我以為我可以在那裡轉。

► 逆向行使

問 Do you know you are going the wrong way on the one-way street?
你知道你正在單行道上逆向行駛嗎？

答 Is this a one-way street?
這是單行道？

▶ 闖紅燈

問 Do you know you went through a stop sign back there?
你知道你剛剛在那裡闖紅燈了嗎？

答 I didn't see that sign.
我沒看到標誌。

你還可以這麼說:

▶ That must be a mistake.
一定是個誤會了。

▶ No, I didn't.
沒有，我沒有。

▶ It wasn't me.
那個不是我。

▶ 行人違規

問 You cannot jaywalk across the rails.
你不可以穿越鐵路。

答 Sorry. I didn't notice the sign.
抱歉，我沒有注意到標誌。

你還可以這麼說:

► Please don't write me a ticket.
請不要開罰單給我。

► Please forgive me this time.
請原諒我這一次。

► 行車勸導

➪ You have to obey all signs and speed limits.
你要遵守所有的號誌及速限。

➪ Do you know the laws of the traffic?
你知道交通規則嗎？

➪ You should wait for a green light.
你應該等綠燈（亮了再走）。

➪ You are going the wrong way on a one-way street.
你正在單行道上逆向行駛。

➪ You have to fasten the seat-belt.
你要繫安全帶。

➪ You'd better watch out when going through an intersection.
當你過路口時，最好小心點。

▶ 超速

問 You were speeding.
你超速了。

答 Really? I was going about eighty, right?
有嗎？我的時速才八十(公里)左右，對吧？

對方可以這麼說:

▶ You were driving faster than the speed limit.
你的車速超越限速了。

▶ 行車速度

問 You were driving at one hundred and twenty kilometers per hour.
你的時速是一百二十公里。

答 Was I?
我有嗎？

對方可以這麼說:

▶ You are driving at least twenty-five kilometers over the limit.

你至少超速了廿五公里。

▶ 警官詢問車禍狀況

問 Is anyone bleeding?
有任何人流血嗎？

答 My friend broke his left leg.
我朋友的左腳斷了。

對方可以這麼說:

▶ It seems no one was injured.

好像沒有人受傷。

▶ Can you move your leg?

你的頭可以動嗎？

▶ Is your car movable?

你的車子可以動嗎？

▶ 警官詢問是否受傷

問 Are you wounded?
你受傷了嗎？

答 I can't move my head.
我的頭不能動。

對方可以這麼說:

▶ Are you all right?

你還好吧？

▶ Where does it hurt?

你哪兒痛？

▶ 車禍受傷

問 Did anyone get injured?
有人受傷嗎？

答 I am bleeding.
我流血了。

你還可以這麼說:

▶ I am in pain.

我好痛。

► I am bleeding right now.

我正在流血。

► My leg hurts.

我的腳痛死了。

► My legs are bleeding in three places.

我的腳有三處地方流血了。

► I think he broke his ankle.

我想他的腳踝斷了。

► 車禍被驚嚇

問 Do you feel all right?
你覺得還好吧？

答 Yes, I'm fine now. I was a little shaken up at first.
是的， 我還好，只是剛開始我有一點被嚇到。

你還可以這麼說:

► I feel dizzy.

我覺得頭暈。

▶ 受傷送醫院

問 Let's get you to the hospital.
我們送你去醫院。

答 Thank you, officer.
謝謝你，警官。

對方可以這麼說:

▶ We can give you a ride home.
我們可以載你回家。

▶ Do you need an ambulance?
你需要叫救護車嗎？

▶ 盤問所需的手續

問 I'll try not to keep you long. I just want a few details, and the rest of the information I can get tomorrow.
我不會耽擱你太久。我只要知道一些細節，其他的資料我可以明天再問。

答 No problem.
沒問題（儘管問）。

你還可以這麼說:

► But I don't remember anything.

但是我什麼都不記得了。

► 盤問車禍發生原因

➪ How did it happen?
事情是怎麼發生的？

➪ When did it happen?
什麼時候發生的？

➪ Which lane were you in?
你在哪個車道？

➪ Which direction were you trying to go?
你要往哪裡去？

➪ How far were you from the car in front of you?
你和你前面的車子距離多遠？

► 車禍後續處理

➪ Try to stay there.
試著留在原地。

➪ Don't move anything.
別移動任何東西。

➪ Please don't touch anything.
請不要碰任何東西。

▶ 記下肇事車禍車牌

問 Did you see the license plate number?
你有看見車牌號碼嗎？

答 Yes, I write down the plate number.
有的，我記下號碼了。

你 還可以這麼說:

▶ My friend already wrote it down.
我的朋友已經把他記下來了。

▶ No, I didn't notice it.
沒有，我沒有注意。

▶ Yes, it's 5461FD.
有的，是5461FD。

▶ 說明肇事原因

問 What's wrong?

怎麼回事？

答 He smashed into me.

他撞到我了。

你還可以這麼說:

▶ The other driver hit my car.

有一部車撞上我的車。

▶ Another driver hit my car and drove away.

另外一個駕駛撞上我的車還逃逸。

▶ 承認肇事

問 Did you hit that old woman?

你剛剛撞倒老婦人嗎？

答 I'm sorry, officer, but I didn't mean to run a red light.

抱歉，警官，但我不是故意要闖紅燈的。

你還可以這麼說:

- But I didn't do it on purpose, officer.
  但是我不是故意的，警官。
- If I didn't stop, I would run into the back of that car.
  如果我不停車，我就會撞上那部車的後面。

▶ 請求不要開罰單

問 I have to give you a ticket!
我必須開你一張罰單！

答 Can't you forgive me this time?
你不能原諒我這一次嗎？

你還可以這麼說:

- This is not my fault. You couldn't give me a ticket.
  這不是我的錯，你不能開我罰單。
- Oh, no！
  喔，慘了！

超簡單的旅遊英語

雅致風靡　典藏文化

親愛的顧客您好，感謝您購買這本書。即日起，填寫讀者回函卡寄回至本公司，我們每月將抽出一百名回函讀者，寄出精美禮物並享有生日當月購書優惠！想知道更多更即時的消息，歡迎加入"永續圖書粉絲團"

您也可以選擇傳真、掃描或用本公司準備的免郵回函寄回，謝謝。

傳真電話：（02）8647-3660　　電子信箱：yungjiuh@ms45.hinet.net

姓名：	性別：　□男　□女
出生日期：　年　月　日	電話：
學歷：	職業：
E-mail：	
地址：□□□	
從何處購買此書：	購買金額：　元
購買本書動機：□封面 □書名 □排版 □內容 □作者 □偶然衝動	
你對本書的意見： 內容：□滿意□尚可□待改進　編輯：□滿意□尚可□待改進 封面：□滿意□尚可□待改進　定價：□滿意□尚可□待改進	
其他建議：	

剪下後傳真、掃描或寄回至「22103新北市汐止區大同路

您可以使用以下方式將回函寄回。

您的回覆，是我們進步的最大動力，謝謝。

① 使用本公司準備的免郵回函寄回。

② 傳真電話：（02）8647-3660

③ 掃描圖檔寄到電子信箱：

yungjiuh@ms45.hinet.net

沿此線對折後寄回，謝謝。

廣告回信
基隆郵局登記證
基隆廣字第056號

2 2 1 - 0 3

雅典文化事業有限公司　收

新北市汐止區大同路三段194號9樓之1

雅致風靡　典藏文化